Wishbone walked around his yard.

He was almost ready to go back inside. Suddenly, something made the fur on his back stand up. He wondered what it was. He listened. He sniffed. Nothing. And yet . . .

Something is wrong, he thought. *I have a spooky feeling, as if something is watching me.*

Wishbone took a few steps. He almost heard something. He was sure of it. He looked all around. Nothing except the darkness.

Wishbone took a few more steps. He had the odd feeling that *something* was walking along with him, just out of his sight.

Books in The SUPER Adventures of **WISHBONE**™ series:

Wishbone's Dog Days of the West
The Legend of Sleepy Hollow
Unleashed in Space
Tails of Terror

Books in The Adventures of **WISHBONE**™ series:

Be a Wolf!
Salty Dog
The Prince and the Pooch
Robinhound Crusoe
Hunchdog of Notre Dame
Digging Up the Past
The Mutt in the Iron Muzzle
Muttketeer!
A Tale of Two Sitters
Moby Dog
The Pawloined Paper
Dog Overboard!
Homer Sweet Homer
Dr. Jekyll and Mr. Dog
A Pup in King Arthur's Court
The Last of the Breed
Digging to the Center of the Earth
Gullifur's Travels
Terrier of the Lost Mines*
Ivanhound*

*coming soon

TAILS OF TERROR

Edited by Kevin Ryan
and Pam Pollack

WISHBONE™ created by Rick Duffield

Big Red Chair Books™, *A Division of Lyrick Publishing*™

This book is a work of fiction. The characters, incidents, and dialogues are products of the authors' imagination and are not to be construed as real. Any resemblance to actual events or persons, living or dead, is entirely coincidental.

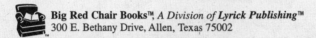 **Big Red Chair Books**™, *A Division of Lyrick Publishing*™
300 E. Bethany Drive, Allen, Texas 75002

©1999 Big Feats Entertainment, L.P.

Edited by Kevin Ryan and Pam Pollack

Copy edited by Jonathon Brodman

Continuity editing by Grace Gantt

Cover design/photo composition by Lyle Miller

Interior illustrations by Jane McCreary, Lyle Miller, Don Punchatz, Arvis Stewart, and Kathryn Yingling

Wishbone photograph by Carol Kaelson

Library of Congress Catalog Card Number: 99-62796

ISBN: 1-57064-480-2

First printing: September 1999

10 9 8 7 6 5 4 3 2 1

For Natasha, Misha, and Kevie, who love scary stories
—Kevin Ryan

To Kevin, with thanks for the inspiration
—Pam Pollack

Contents

FROM THE BIG RED CHAIR . . .

Oh . . . hi! Wishbone here. You caught me right in the middle of some of my favorite things—books. Let me welcome you to THE SUPER ADVENTURES OF WISHBONE. In each of these books, I have adventures with my friends in Oakdale and imagine myself as a character in one of the greatest stories of all time. This story takes place in the fall, when Joe is fourteen and he and his friends are in the eighth grade—during the second season of my television show. In *TAILS OF TERROR*, I imagine I'm different characters from a collection of eight classic ghost tales. In each one, I'm challenged to face evil spirits, unexplained events, and a visit to the netherworld!

You're in for a real treat, so pull up a chair, grab a snack, and sink your teeth into *TAILS OF TERROR!*

Tails of Terror

1

"Grrrreen Tea"

by Brad Strickland

Inspired by "Green Tea"
by J. Sheridan Le Fanu

Illustrated by Kathryn Yingling

*W*hat a Halloween!

Wishbone lay in the study in his big red chair, thinking about the holiday. First, a few days ago, someone had played tricks on people in Oakdale. Wishbone and his best friend, Joe Talbot, had found the trickster and stopped him. Then today, Joe and his close friends, David Barnes and Samantha Kepler, had won first prize in a scavenger hunt at the old, spooky Murphy house.

The Jack Russell terrier yawned. All the excitement of the past few days had finally come to an end. The last trick-or-treater had left the Talbot house, on Forest Lane. Joe and his mom, Ellen, were almost ready to turn in. Wishbone also thought it was nearly time for him to go to sleep.

"Joe," Ellen called from upstairs, "please turn off the porch light before you go to bed."

"All right, Mom," Joe answered from the living room.

Wishbone jumped off his chair. "I'll help! I'll help! On my way, Joe!" He dashed to the front door. The light switch was far above his head. Wishbone made a big jump. He missed. "Why are the switches always so high?" Though Wishbone was strong—and handsome, too, with his white coat and black and brown spots—he could not reach the switch.

"I'll get it, buddy," Joe said, as he walked toward the door. He clicked off the light.

Wishbone grinned at Joe. "I probably would have reached it with another jump, but thanks!"

Joe leaned over to scratch Wishbone's ears. "It's late. I think I'll go up to bed. Are you coming, Wishbone?"

Wishbone shook his head. "In a little while, Joe. This is still Halloween. The brave dog has to be extra careful tonight to protect the family."

After Joe went upstairs, Wishbone walked through the Talbot house. His keen ears listened for strange sounds, and his sensitive nose sniffed for strange smells. His nails clicked on the wood floors.

Wishbone ended his guard patrol in the kitchen. "The fearless dog has checked the area. Everything is clear. Ten o'clock, and all's well! Now, I'd better go outside and check out the yard. Halloween's tricks and treats often happen outdoors."

He hurried through his doggie door. He stepped outside and took a deep sniff.

"Hmm . . ." he said to himself. "It's a misty, cool night. Very dark. I smell dry autumn leaves, and carved pumpkins, and candy that trick-or-treaters have carried by the house. But everything is quiet."

Wishbone walked around the yard. He was almost ready to go back inside. Suddenly, something made the fur on his back stand up. He wondered what it was. He listened. He sniffed. Nothing. And yet . . .

Something is wrong, he thought, *I have a spooky feeling, as if someone is watching me.*

Wishbone took a few steps. He almost heard something. He was sure of it. He looked all around. Nothing except the darkness.

Wishbone was a brave dog, but right now he was worried. What if some bad thing was hiding around one side of the house? It might scare Joe or Ellen! He took a few more steps. He had the odd feeling that *something* was walking along with him, just out of his sight.

Wishbone kept walking and stopping. He looked all around, but he could see no one, nothing. He walked again. Every time he moved, he felt that *something* followed him.

Wishbone stood very still. He sniffed the air. "I don't like this! It's creepy. And it reminds me of something. What is it? Let me see. . . . Someone is walking. Some invisible thing follows him. The walker gets more and more nervous. Oh, of course! This is just like a spooky short story written by the Irish writer J. Sheridan Le Fanu! What's the title? . . . Oh, I've got it! 'Green Tea'!"

J. Sheridan Le Fanu was an Irish writer who lived from 1814 to 1873. He wrote mysteries, vampire tales, and ghost stories. Many people think Le Fanu was the very best writer of ghost stories in his time.

Standing outside in the dark, Wishbone began

to imagine *he* was Dr. Martin Hesselius, from "Green Tea." The doctor had seen many strange and frightening things. But he was not ready for the adventure he was about to have! The year was 1830. The place was a fancy mansion in London, where Lady Mary was having a party. . . .

Dr. Martin Hesselius liked parties. He enjoyed the special foods, and he also liked to watch people. He was doing just that at Lady Mary's party.

Lady Mary came over to the doctor, smiling. "Hello, Dr. Hesselius. Would you mind speaking with one of my guests? He wants to meet you."

With a twinkle in his brown eyes, Dr. Hesselius nodded from the chair where he sat. "Yes. He is a tall, thin man. He has brown hair, and he wears glasses. I believe he is a minister or a professor."

Lady Mary's eyes grew wide. "Why, yes! How clever you are. Mr. Jennings *is* tall and thin. He has brown hair, too, and he once was a college teacher. How did you know?"

Dr. Hesselius twitched his black nose. "I saw the man looking at me earlier. He wanted to speak, but he was too shy. He has a serious look about him. I guessed that he might be either a minister or some kind of teacher."

A servant came over with a tray of snacks. Lady Mary put several of them on the doctor's plate. She said, "He is a retired university professor. Until recently, he was a popular speaker in his hometown of Kenlis.

15

Poor man, he has come down with some illness that keeps him from speaking in public. He would like your advice."

"Then please introduce us," Dr. Hesselius said.

Lady Mary went to look for Professor Jennings. She came back a few minutes later with the man. Dr. Hesselius stood up on his chair. "Here we are," Lady Mary said. "Dr. Martin Hesselius, I would like you to meet Mr. Robert Lynder Jennings."

"How do you do?" Dr. Hesselius said politely.

"I am not very well," said Mr. Jennings with a weak smile. "I hope you are well, however."

"I am, indeed, thank you," Dr. Hesselius said. He looked carefully at Mr. Jennings. *Here is a man in good health,* the doctor thought. *Yet he has a problem. His illness is not of the body. It must be a sickness of the mind . . . or of the spirit.*

With a cough, Mr. Jennings said, "I have read some of your books, Doctor. What interests me is that you write about the mind, as well as the body."

"Are you seeking my advice as a doctor?" asked Dr. Hesselius.

"Well . . . I want to speak with you," Mr. Jennings said.

Dr. Hesselius jumped down from his chair. He landed lightly on his four paws. "Let us go outside onto the balcony," he said. "It will be cooler and more private there."

The two of them stepped away from the crowded party that was going on. They went onto a curved balcony. The night was dark.

"Tell me of your trouble," Dr. Hesselius said.

Mr. Jennings shivered. "I am being haunted," he said in a low voice.

"Ah," said Dr. Hesselius.

"You do not think that is strange?" Mr. Jennings asked.

Dr. Hesselius chose his words carefully. "Yes. Strange things can happen to the mind and the spirit. Tell me about the haunting."

Mr. Jennings looked around nervously. "Not here! Not at night! Wait till tomorrow—when we are in the daylight! Then I will tell you. At night, I am too afraid to speak of it! Perhaps you could visit me. While I am in London, I am staying on Blank Street. I will give you the address."

"Tomorrow, then," said Dr. Hesselius. He looked up at the tall man. He thought, *Whatever haunts you is dangerous. It may not be "real" to others. But to you, it is real and might kill you.* He could hardly wait to hear the man's story.

What was that? Wishbone spun around. He had heard something! The sound came from next door—from the yard of his neighbor, Wanda Gilmore. Wishbone took a few careful steps toward the sound. It was a soft rustle. It came from high up—from the limbs of a fir tree.

Wishbone barked sharply. "Who's there?"

No answer came. For a long time, Wishbone stood still, listening in the quiet of the dark night. He was no longer sure he had heard anything. Maybe his ears were playing tricks on him.

Or maybe not. Wishbone remembered "Green Tea." He recalled the strange story that Dr. Hesselius heard when he visited Mr. Jennings. . . .

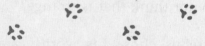

The day was foggy. Dr. Hesselius jumped down from the passenger's compartment of a horse-drawn carriage. He carried a copy of one of his books in his mouth. He trotted down the street until he found the house where Mr. Jennings was staying. Then he knocked softly on the door.

After a moment, a butler came. "Yes, sir?"

It was hard for Dr. Hesselius to speak with the book in his mouth. "Thif if for Mifter Jenningf. I am Dr. Heffeliuf."

"Dr. Heffeliuf?" asked the butler.

"Weed my wips," the doctor said. "Dr. *Heffeliuf.*"

"Oh—Dr. *Hesselius!*" the butler said. "Mr. Jennings is expecting you. Please come in."

The butler led Dr. Hesselius to a cozy study. With relief, the doctor leaped into a chair and opened his mouth. He dropped the book onto a desk. While the butler went to find Mr. Jennings, the doctor looked around. Other books lay on the desk. He had read some of them. One was by a writer named Swedenborg. Dr. Hesselius noticed that it lay open. He began to read.

He scratched his left ear with a hind foot. The book told about invisible spirits that sometimes came to Earth. Those spirits were like ghosts, because they did not have physical bodies. But while ghosts once had bodies and then had died, these spirits had always been invisible beings from another world.

Dr. Hesselius sensed someone standing behind him. He spun around and almost yipped in surprise. "Mr. Jennings!"

The tall man was pale. He patted his face with a handkerchief. "I am sorry. The book you are holding upsets me. Yet I cannot help but read it again and again."

"I brought you a copy of one of my own books. It might be helpful," the doctor said.

"Thank you," Mr. Jennings said. He sat in a chair near the doctor. "I promised to tell you my story. I hope you will not think I am insane."

"Tell me about your problem," the doctor said.

Mr. Jennings leaned back in his chair. "It started three years ago," he said. "I was writing a book myself then. I had read that one by Swedenborg. I wanted to write a book that would argue against the existence of spirits. I spent long hours studying and writing."

Dr. Hesselius lay down and rested his jaw thoughtfully on his paws. "And you drank quite a bit of coffee, didn't you? Or was it tea?"

Mr. Jennings looked surprised. "Why, yes—green tea," he said. "It kept me awake and let me read or write for hours at a time. I drank a great deal of it. How did you know?"

"I will tell you later," the doctor said. "When did you begin to feel haunted?"

Taking a deep breath, Mr. Jennings told his story. It began on a dark night. He had been visiting a friend. He took a horse-drawn bus home. At first, many people were on the bus. Then, one by one, all the passengers got off. Finally, only Mr. Jennings and the driver were left.

"Then I saw them," Jennings said. "Two little spots of red light. I was sitting near the back of the bus, and they were up in the front corner."

"What did they look like?" Dr. Hesselius asked.

Mr. Jennings frowned. "Two round, little glowing red spots, about two inches apart. They were very low down, on the floor. I was curious. I got up from my seat and moved forward slowly. I came near them and bent over. To my horror, I realized the spots were eyes."

"Not human eyes," said Dr. Hesselius, feeling the fur on his neck rise.

With a shiver, Mr. Jennings said, "No. They were the eyes of a . . . a creature. It looked like a monkey. Yet its eyes looked more like those of a cat."

Dr. Hesselius felt like growling. "A cat! Describe this thing, please!"

Mr. Jennings groaned. "Its eyes were angry and glaring. Its mouth was a thin slash across its face, with sharp teeth grinning at me. Its dark gray hair was horrible—greasy, patchy, and spiky. I heard it hiss. It was laughing at me! It had an evil laugh! And its eyes— its eyes showed a frightening intelligence! It was not really a monkey, but some terrible, evil thing that wanted to harm me! It snapped those ugly teeth. I was so afraid that I shouted to the driver to stop. I paid him and jumped off the bus. Then I hurried the rest of the way home on foot."

"That was not the last time you saw the creature, was it?" Dr. Hesselius asked.

"No. I was far away from my home. I ran along Blank Street. I had a very strange feeling. I looked sideways. The dark, gray creature was running on all fours along the top of a wall that went the length of the sidewalk. The thing grinned at me. I had an umbrella in my hand. I swung it at the creature. The umbrella went right through it!" Mr. Jennings gasped. "It was a spirit! And it was haunting me—it *is* haunting me still!"

"What happened next?" asked the doctor, his pointed ears perked up.

"I ran to my house as fast as I could. Once there, I locked the door behind me. I rushed upstairs, shut my bedroom door, and locked it. I went to bed with my heart pounding."

"Did you sleep?"

"After many hours, I finally fell asleep. Then at three in the morning, I woke up suddenly. I opened

21

my eyes, and I saw it! The beast sat right on my chest. It grinned at me. I screamed, and it leaped away!"

Mr. Jennings wiped the sweat pouring down his face and tried to calm himself before going on.

"The butler heard my cries. He came to see what was wrong. Together we searched through the entire bedroom. There was no sign of the creature. I slept no more that night. The next night it came back again."

Dr. Hesselius took a deep sniff. His black nose smelled nothing unusual. "It has not left?"

Shaking his head, Mr. Jennings said, "It comes and goes. At first, it came only at night. I saw it swing on the chandelier in my bedroom. Or it would wake me by touching my face with its cold hands. Then, later on, it began to appear during the day. It would follow me everywhere. Then, a year ago, I was giving a lecture in my hometown of Kenlis. In a full auditorium, the people were listening to me. I glanced down and saw the beast climbing onto the stage where I was standing. No one else there was able to see it—only me!"

"That must have been terrible," Dr. Hesselius said.

"You cannot imagine just how terrible it was. The monster climbed up the podium. It sat on my notes. When I reached for them, it tried to bite my hand. I could not go on speaking. I stood there in front of the audience, shaking and staring. They thought I was ill. . . . I *was* ill. I *am* ill. Since that day, I have not been able to speak to an audience. The beast always comes. I can't even write, for it appears and scares me. I never finished writing my book."

"You have tried to get rid of it?" the doctor asked.

"How can I? It can't be touched—it does not have

23

a real body the way you and I do. No one else can see it. I went to a doctor who told me I was imagining things. But it is *real!* I cannot get rid of that creature. Sometimes it does go away. For as long a time as two or even three weeks I will not see it. But then it always returns."

"Is it here now?" the doctor asked.

"No. I have not seen it for fifteen days."

Dr. Hesselius nodded. "Are you still drinking green tea?"

"Why, yes. I have at least one cup a day."

"Then stop drinking it at once," suggested the doctor. He stood on all fours. "You see, you have a sensitive mind. Most of us can't see this kind of spirit. Others can—and the spirit can sometimes drive them insane. You could not see the thing until you started drinking too much tea. Now it has chosen you to haunt."

"What does it want?" asked Mr. Jennings.

"I do not know. I will have to study that. The old tales say that spirits try to bring people to their world. You see, no one ever returns! Has the creature tempted you to do something odd?"

"Yes," Mr. Jennings said. "I was walking with my niece recently. We were out in the countryside. I saw something beside the path. I had not noticed it before. It was an old well, without a cover over it. I said to my niece, 'That should be covered over.' She asked what I meant, and I pointed at the well. She could not see it! 'It's right there,' I said, pointing. At that moment I saw the horrible beast crawling out of the opening. It waved me toward it. I had the strong feeling it wanted me to jump into the well! And I felt myself wanting to do so!"

"Anything else?" asked Dr. Hesselius.

"Sometimes it whispers to me in my bedroom, late at night. It tells me of a door. Sometimes I imagine I *see* a door, like a door made of fog. It wants me to go through the doorway."

"You must never do what it tells you!" the doctor exclaimed. "The imaginary door and the well are gates between *our* world and the *creature's* world. I will study your case. Will you be in London for long?"

"No. Tomorrow I shall return to Kenlis," said Mr. Jennings. "Please visit me there."

"Very well. I shall come to Kenlis," Dr. Hesselius said. "I will be there in one week. Be strong! Together we can fight this thing."

I must be strong, Wishbone thought. He stood beneath the fir tree outside his house in Oakdale and stared up. He could not smell anything. The strong, piny scent of the tree covered all other odors. He could not see or hear anything, either. Yet, somewhere up in those dark branches, *something* was hiding.

Wishbone sat down. "I can wait you out—whatever you are! This dog won't let you get past!" He felt a little worried, but brave, too. Wishbone knew that being brave did not mean that he felt no fear at all. Only foolish people—or foolish dogs—felt no fear when real danger was around. The brave ones faced their fear and still did what they had to do.

That's me, Wishbone thought. *Brave and ready. Just like Dr. Hesselius, in the story. . . .*

After a week of study, the doctor was ready. He

took a coach to the countryside village of Kenlis, where Mr. Jennings lived.

Dr. Hesselius knocked at Mr. Jennings's door.

The same butler who worked for Jennings in London answered. "Dr. Hesselius!" he said. "Thank heaven you are here! Mr. Jennings is very ill. Please come in."

The butler led the doctor into a gloomy library. Every wall had bookcases from floor to ceiling. The place smelled dusty, like old books. In a moment, Mr. Jennings came in. The doctor was shocked by how thin and sick the man looked.

"The creature is here!" Mr. Jennings said.

"Now? Where?" asked the doctor.

"There! There!" Mr. Jennings pointed to a high shelf. "It crouches there. It snarls at me. The beast knows you, hates you, and wants me to throw you out!"

Dr. Hesselius could see nothing on the shelf except books. "It knows I have been studying ways to get rid of it," he said. "When did it return?"

"The day after your visit in London," Mr. Jennings said. "Oh, I wish you could see it! It is terrifying! No matter where I go, it gets there before me! It just jumped down! Keep it away from me!" Mr. Jennings ran behind the doctor.

"Get away!" barked Dr. Hesselius. He could not see anything, but he guessed where the beast was. "Get away from this man!"

"He will not listen to you! Help! It is climbing onto me!"

Dr. Hesselius watched as Mr. Jennings slapped at something invisible on his leg. "Be strong!" the doctor shouted.

27

Mr. Jennings pointed to a corner of the room. "Do you see it? Do you?"

With the fur standing up on his back, Dr. Hesselius said, "I see only the books! What do *you* see?"

"The imaginary door!" screamed Mr. Jennings. "It is open! Ugh! The nasty creature is pulling at my trousers leg! It wants to pull me through the door!"

In a forceful voice, Dr. Hesselius roared, "By the powers of Good, I demand that you leave this man alone!"

Mr. Jennings stumbled toward a chair. He fell into it. "It has jumped off me," he said. "Now it has climbed back onto the shelf. The door is fading away, like fog. The monster shakes its fists at me and chatters wildly. I shall go out of mind! Can you get rid of it?"

"Not tonight," Dr. Hesselius said. "Its powers are strongest at night. You must rest now."

Mr. Jennings shuddered. "Rest! I am afraid even to lie down! It may do something terrible to me while I am asleep!"

The doctor tried to make him feel better. "You must sleep and grow stronger. We will have to work hard tomorrow." He lifted a paw. "Mr. Jennings, *you* somehow accidentally called this spirit into our earthly world. With my help, you can send it back where it belongs. Tomorrow we will face the creature in the daylight, when it is weak. We must force it to go back through its evil door alone! You will need all your courage and all your strength. I can give you the right words to say, and I can tell you the things you must do tomorrow, but only you can say and do them. So take my advice—and sleep."

That night, Dr. Hesselius stayed in a guest room.

He thought about what he must do to fight the evil beast. At last he slept.

Dr. Hesselius woke up with a start. He heard noises—strange scraping, bumping noises. The doctor leaped out of bed. He rang for the butler. Then he got dressed. When the butler opened the door, Dr. Hesselius said, "Quickly, tell me—did you make anything for Mr. Jennings to drink before he went to bed?"

"No, sir," said the butler. "But he rang for me at one o'clock. He asked me to bring him one cup of tea, sir."

Dr. Hesselius felt cold. The clock beside his bed showed it was three in the morning. "Hurry! We must get to his bedroom!"

The sounds grew louder as they raced down the hall. The butler turned pale when he heard Mr. Jennings inside his bedroom. Mr. Jennings was screaming. His voice was terrified and hoarse. He screamed, *"Aaaahh!"*

"What is happening?" the butler asked.

"Open the door! Hurry! Open it!" shouted Dr. Hesselius.

The butler tried to turn the knob. "It is locked!"

Mr. Jennings's screams from inside the room grew louder. Dr. Hesselius wished he could bite right through the wood. "Quickly," he said, "break down the door! Do it now!"

The butler slammed his body hard against the door—once, twice, three times. The door flew open, just as everything went quiet.

Dr. Hesselius trotted into the bedroom. "Jennings?"

No answer. "Quick!" the doctor said to the butler. "Light a candle!"

As the candle gave off a dim light, Dr. Hesselius heard a fading scream. For just an instant, in the far corner of the room, he thought he saw a door. It was a misty door that closed silently. The scream was suddenly cut off! The door disappeared like fog.

Dr. Hesselius dashed to the corner, his nose to the floor. He could smell Mr. Jennings's scent. It was as though Mr. Jennings had been erased from this world.

Dr. Hesselius inspected the bedroom with sadness. Both of its windows were locked on the inside, just as the bedroom door had been. Mr. Jennings was nowhere in the room. Books had been torn and scattered. Pictures had been ripped from the walls. The bedsheets lay in a tangled heap on the floor.

"This is impossible," the butler said. "How could Mr. Jennings have left? He didn't go through the doorway or the windows!"

Dr. Hesselius saw a cup on the floor. He sniffed it. "No," he said grimly. "Mr. Jennings has gone through

a gate that you could not see. I am afraid he has disappeared into the creature's world." He sighed. "We will
never see him again." The cup at his feet smelled
strongly of . . . green tea.

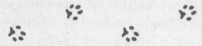

Wishbone shivered, suddenly thinking of the
evil spirit in the story. Was anything bad going to
happen in Oakdale? Was something really watching
him now?

Then he heard the rustle again! A dark shape
leaped from the branches of the fir tree!

Wishbone jumped back, startled. The shape hit
the ground with a thud. Then it hissed.

Wishbone blinked. A cat? A *cat!*

"You furry little fiend!" Wishbone barked.

The shape ran into his neighbor's yard.

Wishbone dashed after it!

The chase was on!

Tails of Terror

2

"The Open Doggie Door"

by Michael Anthony Steele

Inspired by "The Open Door"
by Margaret Oliphant

Illustrated by Don Punchatz

$\mathcal{T}$he chase led to his neighbor Wanda Gilmore's yard.

"Here, kitty, kitty, kitty," Wishbone said. The terrier peeked around a bush that lay between his yard and her yard. "You can run, but you can't hide."

Although it was dark, a nearby streetlight lit up Wanda's front yard. Wanda lived next door to Wishbone and the Talbots. Her white house had bright pink trim. To Wishbone, Wanda's home looked like a life-sized playhouse. Her yard was colorful, too. It had colorful flowers, statues, and pink-plastic flamingos. The thin, auburn-haired woman certainly knew how to liven up a neighborhood.

On this Halloween night, however, Wanda's house seemed more odd than ever. When Wanda was really interested in something, she put all her energy into it. And Halloween was no exception. She had covered her odd house with almost every spooky decoration possible. Smiling jack-o'-lanterns, fake cobwebs, and cardboard skeletons were attached to the house and scattered about the yard. Even her pink-plastic flamingos wore tiny Halloween masks.

Wishbone crept up to a couple of the flamingos.

"Hey," he said to the tall pink birds, "did any of you see a black cat go by here?" The plastic birds didn't answer. They just stared blankly through their masks toward Wanda's house.

Wishbone followed their gaze. He remembered why they were facing in that direction. Earlier that night, Wanda had been part of the scavenger hunt sponsored by Oakdale Sports & Games. It was the local sporting-goods store. Wanda had closed off a large area of her porch with black plastic. There she had set up a shooting gallery for the kids as part of the hunt. Pointing the way to the gallery were the flamingos. Wanda had set them up on the lawn so they formed a path leading to the side porch entrance.

When Wishbone followed some of the flamingos' gazes, he saw the rest of the plastic birds all lined up. They seemed frozen like soldiers in a single-file march toward Wanda's porch. At the very front of the line, Wishbone spotted what he was looking for—the black cat. It was sitting next to the porch. It casually licked at one of its paws.

Wishbone looked back at the line of flamingos. It was as if the birds really had told Wishbone where the cat was, after all.

"Thanks," Wishbone said to the pink birds. The terrier took off after the black cat. "Thought you could get away, did you?" Wishbone barked at the feline.

Looking a bit startled, the cat locked its eyes on the approaching dog. Then it quickly darted inside the enclosed porch.

"Bad move, whiskers!" Wishbone barked. "You just trapped yourself."

Wishbone ran up to the porch entrance. He looked up at the open doorway. Steps led to the porch. On each side of the steps, two jack-o'-lanterns sat on poles. The doorway itself was almost completely dark. Only a faint, orange glow came from inside the enclosed area.

Wishbone peered at the darkness on the other side of the doorway. "I don't know about this," the terrier said. "This doorway looks pretty creepy. In fact, it's almost as strange as another doorway I know about. It's just like a doorway in a very spooky story called 'The Open Door'!"

"The Open Door" is a story that was written about 1852 by a woman named Margaret Oliphant. Born in Scotland, she was a writer who later moved to London, England. There she wrote many stories and serialized novels for *Blackwood's Magazine*. Margaret Oliphant wrote many works of both fiction and nonfiction. Some people think that her stories of the supernatural are among her best work.

Wishbone imagined himself to be Colonel Henry Mortimer, from "The Open Door." Colonel Mortimer had just moved to a new house with his wife, nine-year-old son, and butler.

The house sat atop a small hill near Edinburgh, Scotland. It was a big place, with two stories. The towering walls were made of large brown stones. A gate stood at the entrance to his property. The house overlooked fields and forests. It was also near the ruins of a much older house. In those ruins, only a few moss- and vine-covered stone walls remained standing. And a single door frame.

Colonel Mortimer trotted up the narrow, dark road that led to his house. The cold winter wind ruffled his whiskers. Tiny snowflakes fell from the sky and landed on his long brown coat and black hat.

Normally, the colonel's tail would be wagging as he made his way home from work. Now, however, he had no reason at all to be in a merry mood.

While he was at work, he had received an urgent message from his wife. It seemed that his son, Roland, had become very ill. Their new doctor, Dr. John Simson, had examined the boy and said he had a brain fever. From the tone of his wife's message, Colonel Mortimer knew that his son's condition was serious.

The colonel ran up to the house as fast as his four feet could carry him. He came to the large front door. He quickly scratched on it with his nails. The family butler, Bagley, opened the door. Colonel Mortimer didn't even greet the small man or let Bagley take his hat and coat. Instead, he immediately trotted up the stairs leading to Roland's bedroom. He had to see his son as soon as possible.

Colonel Mortimer stepped into his son's room. Roland was lying in bed. His wife was sitting by the boy's side. The child's skin looked as white as a sheet. Sweat matted his brown hair to his forehead. His eyes were the only part of him that didn't seem sick. They looked like blazing lights shining from his pale face.

The colonel took off his hat and coat. He placed his front paws on the bed.

"He's been asking for you," the colonel's wife, Kate, said. Her blond hair looked a bit messy. She must have been sitting with the boy for some time.

"Father," the boy said. A small smile touched his lips. "I knew you would come!" Roland turned to his mother. "Leave us, please," he said. "I would like to speak with Father alone."

The colonel looked at his wife. "It's all right, Kate." He could tell she was not happy about leaving her sick son, but she left the room, anyway. After she was gone, and the bedroom door was shut, Roland turned to his father.

"They would not let me speak," he said. "Dr. Simson treated me as if I were a fool. You know I am not a fool, Father."

"Yes, yes, my boy. I know," the colonel said. "But you are ill, and being quiet is necessary."

"But I'm not ill," the boy said. He sat up quickly. "I decided to follow Dr. Simson's advice until you came home. I didn't want to frighten Mother. But I tell you, Father," he said, almost jumping out of bed, "it's not an illness I have—it's a secret!" His eyes were wilder than ever.

For a moment, Colonel Mortimer believed the fever had completely taken over the boy. Then he saw the truth in Roland's eyes. The colonel placed a paw on Roland's hand.

"What is this secret?" the colonel asked.

A sad expression came over Roland's face. The boy lay back on the bed. He stared at the ceiling. "Father, as

I was riding my pony tonight, I heard someone in the ruins," he said. "It was someone who has been badly mistreated."

"Well, who is this somebody?" the colonel asked. "Who has been mistreating him? We shall soon put a stop to that."

"Ah," said Roland, "but it is not so easy as you think. I don't know *who* it is. I heard a cry, but I saw no one." The boy rubbed his forehead. "Oh, if you could hear it, Father, it is horrible." The boy frowned. "The doctor thinks that I *dreamed* it."

"Are you quite sure you haven't dreamed it, Roland?" the colonel asked. "These things happen, you know."

"Dreamed it?" Roland sat up again. "The pony heard it, too," he said. "She jumped as if she had been shot. Did the pony dream it?"

"Well, what did the cry sound like?" the colonel asked.

"It was terrible," the boy replied. "It was the cry of a young boy. He kept calling for his mother."

"Surely," the colonel said, "it must be a child who was playing in the ruins and got lost."

"But, Father," Roland said, "suppose it *wasn't* some lost child. Suppose it wasn't even alive!"

Colonel Mortimer couldn't believe his ears. "Are you telling me it is a ghost?" he asked.

"Surely you've heard people tell stories of how the old ruins are haunted." He grabbed his father's paw. "Besides, I wish you had heard it," the boy said. "Whatever it is, it is something in trouble." He squeezed his father's paw tighter. "Oh, Father, it is in terrible trouble!"

The colonel didn't know what to say. "What do you want me to do?" he asked.

"'Father will know,'" Roland said. "That is what I kept saying to myself—'Father will know.' Oh, Father, it's out there all by itself in the ruins with nobody to help it. I can't bear it! I can't bear it!" Roland placed his face in his hands and cried.

Colonel Mortimer felt terrible to see his son so upset. "But, Roland, what can I do?"

"It will be there now—I'm sure it will be there all night. Oh, think, Father, think if it were me. I can't rest for thinking of it. You go and offer help. Mother can take care of me."

Roland called to his mother, and soon she entered the room. The colonel walked slowly toward the bedroom door.

The colonel *had* heard stories about how the ruins were haunted. However, he hadn't believed them. It seemed that every village had some old building or graveyard that was said to be haunted by ghosts or spirits. The colonel wasn't the type to believe in such things. But he was troubled that his son *did* believe in them. It was even more troubling that Roland wanted his father to help this ghost somehow. Colonel Mortimer was not superstitious, but one thing was for sure. He would have to go and investigate the ruins for his son's sake.

"Creepy doorway or not," Wishbone said, "I have to go in there." He gazed into Wanda's covered porch. "I have to think of my canine duties. There's a cat in there that needs to be taught a lesson. It can't be allowed to go around trying to scare cute little dogs!"

Wishbone crept up the steps leading toward the doorway. He put one paw onto the porch. He was about to enter the dark area. Suddenly, the cat dashed out of the doorway. It almost ran right into the terrier. The cat raced past Wishbone and darted into the dark shadows of the yard.

Wishbone looked at the running cat. "Watch where you're going, will you?" He turned back toward the doorway. "I'm trying to sneak in here and catch a . . . oh, wait, I'm trying to catch *you*."

Wishbone lifted his paw off the porch. Then he turned to continue his cat chase when an idea came to him. *I wonder what startled that cat so much,* he thought. Wishbone turned back to the porch. *Is there something hiding in there?*

Even though the whole situation seemed spooky, the terrier was curious. Wishbone swallowed hard. Once again, he stepped onto Wanda's porch. This time, instead of just placing one paw on the porch, the dog crept slowly up into the dark place.

Wishbone looked around inside the area. The only bit of light was coming from a grinning jack-o'-lantern on his right. A small orange lightbulb burned inside it. Wishbone looked to his left and saw the large shooting gallery he and the kids had played earlier that night. The large, grinning face of the jack-o'-lantern was projected onto it.

Earlier that night, during the scavenger hunt, Wishbone had seen the shooting gallery when it had been turned on. The gallery was filled with moving metal animals. All the animals had a tiny bull's-eye painted on them. They would zip back and forth when the machine was on. Now that the gallery's power was off, the tiny ducks, foxes, and rabbits stood still.

The terrier looked around the porch. Although it was dark, quiet, and creepy, Wishbone didn't see why the cat should have been so frightened.

"I don't see what's so scary here," Wishbone said. The dog turned and began to leave. "I guess that's why they're called *scaredy-cats.*"

Wishbone was about to leave the porch when he heard a strange sound. The dog froze in his tracks. Slowly, he turned his head toward the shooting gallery. The large game began to shake. The wooden floor beneath the game made a deep rattling noise.

"Uh," Wishbone said, "what was that?"

The game was quivering. It was as if someone was

physically shaking it. But there was no one there. The game was shaking by itself.

The terrier slowly backed away from the game and moved toward the doorway. "Maybe there's such a thing as scaredy-*dogs,* too," he said with a slight shakiness in his voice.

As Wishbone slowly made his way outside, he thought of the story "The Open Door." The shaking game was just as creepy as what Colonel Mortimer had found in the ruins near his house.

"Speaking of houses," Wishbone said, "maybe I should get away from this one!"

Wishbone quickly leaped through the doorway and ran out into the dark night.

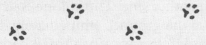

Colonel Mortimer and his butler, Bagley, made their way through the cold night. When they came near the ruins, the colonel shone his lantern toward the high stone walls. The light formed a long beam that cut right through the falling snow. Bagley stood behind the colonel, holding another lantern. Bagley couldn't hold his lantern too steady, so his light jumped from spot to spot. He was a much more superstitious man than the colonel, and his shaking arm was proof of his nervousness. He was not at all happy about being at the ruins.

"Do you still want to follow me, my man?" Colonel Mortimer asked, as he held on tightly to the lantern's handle. The colonel turned to see the butler nodding his head. From Bagley's expression, he didn't seem too sure.

Slowly, the two crept even closer to the dark ruins. The light from their lanterns danced across the old vine-covered stone walls. At one time, a large house had stood there. But now, only crumbling walls were left.

To the left of the ruins was a single stone door frame. The colonel shone his light upon it. There didn't seem to be anything odd about the doorway. It was covered with moss and vines, just like the rest of the ruins. What did make the door frame unusual was that it stood all by itself, away from the crumbling walls. It wasn't attached to anything.

The two men approached the doorway cautiously. They examined it as the light from their lanterns washed over it. The colonel walked through it and examined the other side. The colonel saw a dark shape huddled near the ground. Immediately, he aimed his lantern toward it. It was only a small berry bush.

Both the colonel and Bagley stood at the open doorway. There was nothing odd. They stood there a moment longer. The cold winter wind blew through the colonel's fur. Thick snowflakes fell all around him.

As the colonel was about to turn and investigate the rest of the ruins, he suddenly heard a loud cry. It came from under the colonel's paws. Both the colonel and Bagley sprang backward on different sides of the doorway. Colonel Mortimer was so surprised that his lantern slipped from his grasp and fell to the ground. The light went out. There was only darkness on his side of the doorway.

There was another sound, a low moaning coming from the ground. The moaning slowly grew to a low cry full of suffering and pain.

"What is it, sir?" Bagley yelled from the other side of the doorway.

"I can't tell," the colonel said. "Shine your lantern at the ground below."

Bagley's light lit up the dark doorway. The colonel saw nothing but their own footsteps in the snow.

"Who's there?" the colonel asked. There was no answer, just another weary cry.

Colonel Mortimer stepped closer toward the doorway. He bent his head down to the ground. Maybe he could pick up the crier's scent with his powerful sense of smell. The colonel pawed at the snow until he uncovered a small patch of ground. He smelled the moist earth and the musty smell of the dirt. Nothing more.

As the colonel stood just inside the doorway, something grabbed him.

"I've got him, Colonel!" Bagley shouted. "I've got him!"

"Bagley!" the colonel barked. "It's me!"

Just then, another loud shriek burst from underneath the men. This one was the loudest yet. Bagley let go of the colonel and leaped back in fear. He tripped and almost fell. Bagley's lantern fell to the ground but didn't go out. Luckily, the light of his lantern was still aimed at the doorway. The butler just stood shaking as he stared at the structure.

The colonel turned his attention from Bagley back to the open door. He took a few steps back and listened. His fine sense of hearing was very well tuned that night. The colonel heard the wailing voice moving back and forth in front of the door frame. It was as if someone was pacing.

Then, for the first time, the voice said something understandable. "Mother!" the voice cried. "Oh, Mother!"

Colonel Mortimer's fur stood on end. The voice sounded like a young boy.

"Oh, Mother!" the voice repeated urgently. "Mother, let me in! Oh, Mother, let me in! Please, let me in!"

Still startled, the colonel felt a little relieved. What Roland had said was true. His son didn't have brain fever or some other disease. The voice Roland heard was real.

"Who are you?" Colonel Mortimer asked the strange voice.

There was no reply to his question. The voice continued to cry out and repeat the same phrase. "Oh, Mother, let me in! Oh, Mother, let me in!"

Colonel Mortimer had never been the type of

person who believed in ghosts. But he couldn't explain what was happening. He was hearing the heartbreaking sound of a young boy pleading for his mother to let him in. However, there was no boy visible, and no door to be locked out of.

"Oh, Mother, let me in!" the voice called again. "Oh, Mother, please!"

Colonel Mortimer looked up and he saw a dark silhouette in the doorway. The figure stood just on the other side of the open door.

"Come in!" the colonel shouted at the top of his voice. "Come in! Come in!"

The figure took a step through the doorway. It then began to fall toward the colonel. Colonel Mortimer jumped out of its way. As the figure fell to its knees, the colonel saw that it was Bagley, his butler.

The colonel went to Bagley's side. The figure had not been anything supernatural, after all. The frightened man had fainted.

Then, as suddenly as the voice had appeared, it was gone. Colonel Mortimer looked around the dark and now very quiet ruins. He didn't know what the voice was, but he knew he had to find out—if not for his own curiosity, then for Roland's well-being.

Bagley began to move.

"Come, Bagley." The colonel put a comforting paw on the old man's shoulder. "Let's get you home."

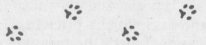

Wishbone sat in Wanda's dark yard. He stared at the doorway leading to Wanda's porch.

"Okay," Wishbone said, "there's nothing *too* creepy here—a nice cool breeze, some jack-o'-lanterns, and . . . oh, yeah . . . a shooting gallery that *moves by itself!*"

Wishbone looked over his shoulder. The black cat sat almost in darkness next to a bush. The cat just looked blankly at Wishbone.

Wishbone turned back toward Wanda's house. He stood and took a step toward the dark doorway. He lifted his nose into the air. Then the terrier took in a few deep sniffs. The place did not smell strange to him. Wanda's porch smelled just the way it always had—like Wanda's porch.

Wishbone turned back to the cat. "We'll have to settle our business later," he said. The dog looked at the open doorway. "In the meantime, there's something strange going on here." The terrier took another step toward the porch. "And since I'm the neighbor-hood watchdog, it's my duty to check it out." He paused. "No matter how creepy it is."

Wishbone thought back to Colonel Mortimer and his first experience at the ruins. And, just like Wish-bone, Colonel Mortimer was going to have to go back to investigate the strange event again.

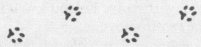

"You've got an epidemic in your house, Colonel Mortimer," Dr. Simson said the next morning. The heavyset man was closing his black bag. He walked out of Bagley's room. "What's the meaning of it all? Not only is your son insisting he heard a voice, but so is your butler." He closed the door to the butler's room. "What's the meaning of it all?" he said again, completely puzzled by what was happening in the household.

"Both Roland and Bagley speak the truth," the colonel said. He trotted beside the doctor as they walked down the upstairs hallway. "I heard the same voice."

Dr. Simson stopped walking. "Then you are in-fected, as well," he said.

The colonel looked up at the doctor. "Come, you can't put us *all* to bed, you know," he said with a short wag of his tail. The colonel hopped onto one of two nearby chairs. "You need to listen and hear *all* of the symptoms of this 'fever.'"

The doctor sat in the other chair. Colonel Mortimer told the man everything that had happened the night before. He told him about the ruins, the doorway, and the strange voice.

"My dear fellow," Dr. Simson said, "your butler told me exactly the same story. It's an epidemic, I tell you. When one person falls victim to this sort of thing, it's quite easy for others to follow."

"Then how do you explain it?" the colonel asked. He was getting annoyed.

"Explaining it is a different matter," the doctor replied. "There's no explaining the crazy thoughts that sometimes come into our brains."

Colonel Mortimer let out a bark. "Then come with me tonight and judge for yourself!"

The doctor laughed. "It would ruin my reputation if people found out that John Simson went ghost-hunting," he said as he stood. "You're imagining this whole thing. It is not wise to encourage something like this. Even if I *did* hear this voice, I wouldn't believe it was a ghost."

The colonel jumped off his chair. "That's what I would have said yesterday," he told the doctor. "But come with me tonight. I have asked Father Moncrieff, our minister, to join me, as well. If you do not believe what you hear, you may put me to bed just like the others."

The doctor began to walk toward the stairs. "Well, Colonel," he said, "you have made your butler quite ill on your trip to the ruins. He lies in his bed terrified beyond belief. And now you want to risk my health and the well-being of Father Moncrieff?" He let out another laugh. "But I will do it. I will meet you at your front gate this evening, after I finish seeing patients."

Colonel Mortimer walked the doctor to the front door and watched him leave. Then he turned and looked toward the stairs that led up to the room of his son, Roland. The colonel didn't know if the doctor and the minister would be able to help him solve the mystery. But he knew he had to try—for Roland's sake.

That night, Colonel Mortimer met Dr. Simson and Father Moncrieff at the front gate of his property. The colonel had to pass the old ruins on the way to the gate, but he hadn't heard anything. He only hoped the voice would be there later. That way, the doctor and the minister could hear it, too.

The colonel greeted the two men. Both carried lanterns and wore heavy coats. Father Moncrieff was a much older man than the doctor or the colonel. He was thin, with a short white beard. Heavy snow was falling that night, just as it had the previous evening. Tiny piles of snow had begun to form on the two men's shoulders and hats.

The three walked from the gate up the narrow road leading to the colonel's house. When they finally neared the ruins, they all moved off the road. The beams from their lanterns washed over the crumbling walls.

The colonel led them to the open door. He didn't have to say a word. He had already told both men the story. They just stood there and waited for something to happen.

After a few minutes passed, Father Moncrieff spoke. "How long do you think we will have to stay here?"

"I'm not sure," the colonel replied.

"I thought so," the doctor said. "It is the same with a séance or other phony ghostly sightings. If a non-believer shows up, nothing happens."

The colonel looked at Father Moncrieff, but he was silent.

Colonel Mortimer didn't know how long they would have to wait. In fact, he didn't even know if the voice would return. The stories he had heard from local villagers claimed the voice cried out every night during the winter months.

Then, in the distance, he heard something. It was the soft sobs and cries of a young boy. It sounded as if the boy was walking toward them. Soon the voice was close enough for the other two men to hear.

"What is that?" Father Moncrieff asked.

The doctor shone his lantern toward the sound of the distant voice. There was nothing to see but trees and the walls of the ruins. The voice got closer and louder.

"That child has no business being out so late," the doctor said.

The three men listened to the approaching voice. It sounded as if someone was walking toward them and was next to the ruins. Both the doctor and the minister tried to locate the voice with their lanterns. But there was nothing. The moans and cries made their way to the open door, then fell silent.

After the sounds stopped, Dr. Simson walked around the ruins and the open door. Colonel Mortimer was sure the doctor was looking for a person who was hiding. Perhaps he thought the colonel had told some-one to hide in the ruins. The doctor continued to search.

The colonel turned his attention to Father Moncrieff. The man just stood there, gazing at the open door. His mouth was slightly open.

Colonel Mortimer was about to speak to him when he heard the voice again. Every sob and every cry was exactly the same as the night before.

When the doctor heard the cries begin again, he rushed back to join the others. "How long does this go on?" he whispered. It was as if he didn't want to interrupt the person making the cries.

The colonel was about to answer when, just like the night before, the cries turned to words.

"Oh, Mother, let me in!" the voice cried. "Oh, Mother, let me in!"

"Let him in?" the doctor asked. "There's not even a door there."

"Oh, Mother, let me in!" the voice said again. "Oh, Mother, let me in! Please let me in!"

"Willie!" a voice said from behind the doctor and the colonel. "Willie! Is that you?"

The two men turned to see Father Moncrieff. The man was very pale. His eyes were wet and glistening, and his mouth was quivering.

"Oh, Mother, let me in!" the voice continued, sounding just as it had the night before. "Mother, please!"

"Willie, if that is you," the minister called again, "if that is you and not a dream, why have you come here?"

For the first time, the colonel noticed a break in the voice's pattern. The voice of the young boy stopped asking for his mother. And unlike the night before, only quiet sobs could be heard.

Colonel Mortimer noticed something else, too. The wind had begun to blow with more fury. The falling snow seemed to grow thicker as it was tossed about. In fact, the snow was falling so heavily that the colonel had to take a few steps closer to the others just to see them.

"Why are you here, Willie?" Father Moncrieff continued. "Your mother is gone with your name on her lips. Do you think she would ever close her door on her own son?" There was no reply in words, only quiet sobs.

The snowstorm increased with unnatural swiftness.

The minister paused a moment. Then he took a step toward the open door. "I forbid you!" he yelled in a commanding voice. "Cry out no more to man. Go home, you wandering spirit! Do you hear me? I who christened you. I who have watched you grow!"

Colonel Mortimer and Dr. Simson stood still and stared at the one-sided conversation. The colonel didn't know how or why, but the minister knew this spirit.

Father Moncrieff took another step closer to the open door. The sobs were beginning to fade. The minister's voice also became more quiet. The colonel could barely hear it over the fiercely blowing wind.

"And her, too," the minister said. "The poor woman you are calling upon is not here. You'll find her in heaven. Go and call against heaven's gate, and not your poor mother's ruined door."

The crying was almost completely silenced in the violent snowstorm. Colonel Mortimer's keen hearing could pick up only a few sobbing breaths.

"Are you hearing me, Willie?" the minister asked. His voice grew louder once more. "Go on! Go to heaven! Are you hearing me?"

Suddenly, the colonel saw something fling itself wildly through the doorway. Colonel Mortimer jumped out of its way, but there was nothing there. One last gust of wind blew through his fur. Then all was still. The snow had stopped falling. The wind was gone. The voice was gone.

For a few minutes, all three men stood in silence. Then Father Moncrieff turned to the others. "I must be going," he said. "It's very late." He turned and started to walk toward the main road.

"How did you know?" Dr. Simson asked, following the minister away from the ruins. He hurried to catch up with the minister. "How did you know the boy's name?"

Father Moncrieff did not answer right away. Instead, he continued toward the road. Colonel Mortimer looked at the open door again. It seemed to him that whoever the voice had belonged to had followed Father Moncrieff's advice. It seemed as if the ghostly cries would be gone for good. The colonel gave two quick wags of his tail before trotting through the snow to catch up with the other men.

When the colonel reached them, the minister spoke. "The young lad's mother was the housekeeper for the home that used to stand there," Father Moncrieff said. "That doorway was the door to the servants' quarters—her door. I was quite familiar with the mother and her child." The minister took a deep breath, then continued. "The boy had left home when he was quite young. When he returned, he learned that his mother had passed away just the day before." He took another breath. "I remember that day very clearly. The young lad was so upset by his mother's death that he threw himself down at the door. He called out loudly, over and over, for her to let him in."

The three reached the main road and walked toward the gate.

"The boy grew older and soon left our fair village, never to be seen again. It would seem, however, that his spirit never left that door," Father Moncrieff said. "That is, until tonight."

"I must admit," Dr. Simson said, "if I hadn't heard it with my own ears, I wouldn't have believed it." He turned to Colonel Mortimer. "I'm not even sure if I believe it now. But what I *do* believe is that your son and butler are not ill."

The colonel wagged his tail. "Thank you very much, Dr. Simson."

Together, the three walked in silence. Neither Dr. Simson nor Colonel Mortimer asked Father Moncrieff any more questions. They walked down the snow-covered road toward the main gate. When they reached it, each went his separate way.

The next day, Colonel Mortimer walked into his son's room. Roland already appeared to be in much better spirits. The colonel trotted over to the boy's bed. He placed his front paws on Roland's bedside.

"All is well, Roland," the colonel said. He wagged his tail slightly. "All is well." Colonel Mortimer told the young boy everything that had happened the night before. He explained that the tortured spirit in the ruins was tortured no more.

The young boy sat up. He placed one of his small

hands on the colonel's paw. "I knew you would find a way, Father." He smiled and lay back down.

The colonel sat with his son for a while longer. Then he quietly left the room. He knew his son would be well in no time at all. As the colonel trotted down the stairs, he realized something else. He had helped his son, just as Father Moncrieff had helped the young boy calling out to his mother. The colonel wagged his tail. It felt good knowing that both young boys' spirits were now at ease.

Wishbone looked into the dark room. He still had only one paw on the porch. After a moment, he looked back at the black cat. The cat still sat in the same place.

"Maybe *you* should go inside again," the terrier said. "Then you could come back and tell me what's in there. What do you say?"

The cat didn't answer. It just sat in Wanda's yard, staring at the dog.

"Any chance?" Wishbone asked.

The cat didn't answer.

Wishbone turned back to the dark porch. "Well, okay," he said, "you're missing out on a lot of . . ."—Wishbone swallowed hard—". . . fun."

The dog quietly hopped onto the porch. He stepped into the dark area. Just as before, the shooting gallery was bathed in the orange light that came from the bulb inside the nearby jack-o'-lantern. Unlike before, however, the gallery wasn't shaking.

"Uh . . ." Wishbone said, "maybe it was just a

small earthquake." He stared at the quiet gallery. "Yep, that must have been what happened!" The dog turned around. He was about to hop off the enclosed porch. "Well, since everything is quiet here . . ."

The shooting gallery began to shake again.

"I had to go and open my big mouth!" the dog said. Wishbone slowly turned toward the shaking game. "Well, I suppose I should check things out," he said in a shaky voice. "I guess this falls under the 'keeping Oakdale safe for humans and dogs alike' part of my canine oath."

Wishbone took a small step toward the machine. As he did, he noticed something strange. The large game seemed to be shaking more near the bottom. It was as if whatever was making the thing shake was behind the machine and near the floor. Wishbone stepped closer.

"Helllooo?" the dog said. "If there is any kind of a ghost or monster behind the game, don't worry." Wishbone stepped closer. "I'm just going to take a quick look behind there and then be on my way." He stepped closer. "Then you can get back to shaking shooting galleries—or whatever it is you do."

Wishbone moved closer. The shooting gallery continued to rumble. The dog had made his way almost to the back of the machine. If there was any *thing* back there, he would soon be able to see it. Wishbone finally reached the back of the game. He stuck out his neck as far as he could. He wanted to see what was behind the game. But he also wanted to be as far away as possible from whatever it was when he saw it.

The bulb from the jack-o'-lantern gave off just

enough light. He wouldn't have any trouble seeing what was behind the large gallery.

Suddenly, the jack-o'-lantern bulb went out. The entire porch was plunged into complete darkness.

"Uh . . ." Wishbone said, "this is not good."

Then, all at once, another light came on. This one came from behind the game itself. The light revealed two large eyes only inches away from Wishbone's face. They were looking directly at him.

"Aaaaaaaaaah!" Wishbone screamed.

"Aaaaaaaaaah!" the second voice screamed.

Wishbone ran outside as fast as he could. He turned back to see his neighbor, Wanda Gilmore, exit right behind him. In one hand, she held a flashlight. In her other hand, she held a white electrical cord. Wishbone thought that cord must have been the one that led to the lightbulb in the jack-o'-lantern. Wanda had probably shaken the game while trying to reach an electrical outlet.

"Wishbone!" Wanda yelled. "You scared me half to death!"

"Uh . . . sorry, Wanda," Wishbone replied. "You see, this cat here . . ."

Wishbone turned to where the cat had been sitting. It was gone. Wishbone looked around and saw the cat moving toward the Talbots' yard. The terrier turned back to Wanda.

"I mean that cat *there* . . ." the dog said.

"Wishbone," Wanda said, "what am I going to do with you?"

Wishbone didn't want to stick around to find out.

"Good question, Wanda," the dog said. He turned

around and headed after the cat. "But the big question is—what am I going to do to that cat for causing all this trouble?"

The cat ran toward a flower bed that separated Wanda's yard from the Talbots' yard. Wishbone took off after it.

I think catching this cat may take all night, he thought to himself.

Wishbone ran a bit faster. "Here, kitty, kitty, kitty!"

Tails of Terror

3

"A New Leash on Life"

by Mary Ryan

Inspired by "The Haunters and the Haunted"
by Edward Bulwer-Lytton

Illustrated by Jane McCreary

ishbone had just chased the black cat off Wanda Gilmore's porch. The terrier ran to the edge of Wanda's garden. Then he stopped and listened. Were those footsteps sneaking up behind him? He whirled around.

Whew! It's just a bunch of dry leaves tumbling across the sidewalk.

A strong wind began to blow up the street. Wishbone sniffed the Halloween night air.

Suddenly, Wishbone became aware of something. "Helllooo!"

He looked up at a nearby tree. A pair of yellow eyes stared back at him. Wishbone growled.

One unwelcome guest detected. One eviction, about to get under way!

From overhead, the cat let out a meow. Wishbone tensed his muscles. *I am a brave hunter of the night,* he thought. *Armed only with an amazing nose and great courage, I shall corner my prey. It will* not *escape!*

Wishbone saw something race down the tree trunk. "Halt! That means you!" Wishbone saw the black cat dash through Wanda's garden. Before he could give chase, a sudden gust of strong wind rattled

windows and shook the trees. Suddenly a weird light flickered inside the Barnes's garage.

What's that?

Wishbone and Joe's good friend David Barnes had a workshop in the garage. There was another blast of wind as Wishbone took a step forward. *There it goes again! On—off. On—off . . .*

Wishbone braced himself against the wind as he crossed the Talbots' yard toward the garage. Wishbone had just reached the corner of the house, when the Barnes's garage door began to rise . . . all by itself.

"Did someone say 'Open Sesame'?" Wishbone walked over and peered inside. "Yoo-hoo! David? Anybody home?"

Nope. The place looks deserted and dark. Then who opened the door?

Puzzled, Wishbone trotted inside to investigate. At the same time, a dark shape slipped past him.

I know that smell, and it's not fresh kibble. In fact, it's the same cat I've been chasing all night! With a bark, Wishbone charged at the shadow.

Behind him, the garage door closed with a bang.

Oh, no! Now I'm the one who's trapped! In a dark and spooky place. With a cat! And . . . what's that?

On the other side of the door, Wishbone heard an eerie sound. It sounded like *tap-tap-tap*. . . . The Jack Russell shivered. "This place is really giving me the creeps! Weird noises . . . a door opening and closing by itself . . . trapped in a spooky place . . ."

The situation reminded Wishbone of a classic ghost story written by an English author with two last names: Edward Bulwer-Lytton! The story he wrote had two names, too: "The Haunters and the Haunted; or The House and the Brain"!

Edward Bulwer-Lytton lived from 1803 to 1873. He was a member of the British Parliament, and he even served as Secretary of State. But he also wrote plays and novels, and he published a number of horror stories.

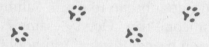

Trapped inside the garage, Wishbone imagined that *he* was the adventurer from "The Haunters and the Haunted." He was a young Englishman with a nose for danger. So, spending the night in a haunted house was right up his alley.

But even *he* wasn't prepared for what was about to happen! The year was 1859. The place: a Victorian home in London . . .

It was a pleasant day in June, 1859, and I was in a fine mood. Her Majesty, Queen Victoria, had been the ruler of England since 1837. London was a busy capital city, full of horse-drawn carriages, fine restaurants, and gossip. And I, a well-bred young gentleman of leisure, loved all three!

Wearing an elegant blue frock coat and striped waistcoat, I strolled through the heart of Knightsbridge. It was a fancy section of the city. I looked up at the beautiful houses and tipped my top hat to well-dressed people I passed by. I recognized one—it was my old college roommate. We stopped to chat, and he told me an amazing story.

My ears pricked up when he spoke of a haunted house on Oxford Street. It was just the sort of adventure I'd been looking for. I knew I *had* to spend the night there!

But when I told him so, my friend placed a hand on my paw. "I beg you, stay away from that house! Several weeks ago, my wife and I rented some rooms there from an old woman. Our reservation was for two nights. But we stayed for only part of one."

"Did you see a ghost?" I asked eagerly.

"We saw nothing. But whenever we passed a certain room, a feeling of great terror gripped us both. It was awful! At last, I told the clerk we could not stay another night—or even another moment!"

"Was she surprised?" I asked.

My friend shook his head. "No. She said few guests stayed a second night, and none a third. Then she added a strange remark: 'They must have been very kind to you.'"

"They? Who's *they?*"

My friend shivered. "'They who haunt the house. They will be the death of me someday—and then I will be with them forever!' Those were the woman's exact words." My friend's face broke out in a nervous sweat. "We paid our bill and left the place within the hour!"

This adventure seemed very tempting. I struggled

71

to control my excitement. *Hauntings? Ghosts? Not a doggone problem for me. Sign me up!*

"I'll bet you a hundred pounds that I can stay there twice as long as you!" I said. Though I lived on an allowance from my rich uncle, he kept me on a pretty tight leash. Since I could never resist a good bet, I always came up a little short . . . on cash.

My friend shook his head. "You are single and carefree. Perhaps all of life seems like an adventure to you. But you may live to regret this."

And I can think of a hundred reasons why I won't!

"Nonsense," I replied. "I will go and see the woman this very day. Me, afraid of some invisible spirits? 'Adventure' is my middle name!"

Finally, he accepted my bet. I went quickly to Oxford Street with a merry heart. When I reached the house, I stood up tall on my hind legs to knock on the door.

Hmm . . . a friendly touch—that knocker is shaped like a serpent's head. Not that I have anything against snakes. . . . Okay, I can't stand snakes!

I took hold of the iron serpent and then let it drop three times. But there was no answer.

Jumping up on a low wall, I peered through the gloomy windows. Inside I saw what looked like musty, moldy rooms. A strange feeling hung over the place, as if the house had secrets it didn't want to tell.

"You will, if I have anything to do with it," I barked. I noticed a For Rent sign by the front door. It had the owner's name on it. I decided to go speak to the owner, Mr. J——. The nice old gentleman listened to what I had to say. Then he agreed to allow me to stay in the house.

"My caretaker died three weeks ago, and no one will rent the place. I shall not charge you anything to stay here. But there is one condition."

There's always a condition, I thought. But I was game. "Just name it," I said, my tongue practically hanging out in my eagerness to begin the adventure.

"Find out what's causing the strange events in my house. If you do, I will be forever in your debt!"

Someone in my *debt? I like the sound of that!* I quickly promised, then offered him my paw. We shook on it, and Mr. J—— gave me the key.

As I walked home to get what I needed, I thought back to my conversation with Mr. J——.

"Let's get this straight. Three weeks ago the caretaker says that 'they' will be the death of her— and now she's dead. Why doesn't this seem as if it's a coincidence?"

But it wasn't in me to spend a lot of time thinking

about unpleasant things. I was carefree and happy-go-lucky. And my fine adventure was close at paw!

At my house, I packed my revolver and my dagger, along with some food and clothing supplies. To keep myself alert, I brought along a book to read. Finally, I set out for the haunted house.

It was a chilly summer night, gloomy and cloudy. I neared the place. The street where it was, which that morning had seemed so lively, was now deserted and dark. A ghostly moon peeked out from behind clouds. I couldn't help but shiver as I guided the key into the lock, opened the front door, and slipped inside.

The place smelled as damp and musty as it looked from outside. I went from room to room on every floor of the house, sniffing in each corner. But I found nothing strange, only the cobwebs that stuck to my whiskers and made me sneeze.

Just my luck, I thought, disappointed. *It must be the ghosts' night off.* Instead, I went back downstairs and headed for the living room. When I got there, my heart lifted as I put down my supplies.

"Oh—someone has lit a fire. Could it be that I have . . . company? Helllooo! Anybody home?"

My bark echoed through the halls. *Perhaps the house only* seems *deserted,* I told myself. *Can "they" stay out of sight for long?*

Suddenly, a footprint formed out of thin air. I stared at it in amazement. It stepped toward me, passed by, then disappeared into a wall. *Ouch! That's* gotta *hurt.*

My fur bristled with excitement at the thought of seeing spooky things. I settled by the fire to wait for some action.

Nearly an hour passed with no further signs of anything unusual. I was about to fetch my book, when a chair scooted out from the wall and seemed to float right in front of me.

"No visible means of support—reminds me of some of my old pals from college!" As I watched, the pale outline of a person began to take shape. The misty form rose and motioned me toward the staircase that led up to the floors above.

Immediately I thought of my friends at the Cosmopolitan Club, a gentlemen's club in the center of London. When it came to doing daring things, I was considered top dog. *Wait till I tell the guys about this adventure. I'll be the talk of London!*

I made sure my weapons were within paw's reach. Then I trotted up the stairs behind the ghostly guide.

At the top of the stairs, the phantom paused. In the blink of an eye, it slipped under a small door. I rushed over and sniffed.

Strange—I unlocked all the doors when I first got here, including this one. I pushed against it with all my strength. But the door wouldn't budge. It was locked tight.

"This *is* odd." Puzzled, I sat down to scratch my ear. "It can't be locked from the inside, unless . . ."

My paw froze next to my ear. Slowly, the door to the room began to swing open!

I peered into the shadowy room. It looked dark and creepy. It smelled as though no one had been inside it for years. With my sharp eyes, I saw long strands of dust swaying from the ceiling. I finally went all the way into the room. A window, its shutters closed, was

set in one wall. But there was no other door, or even a fireplace, through which someone could have entered and opened the door.

My nails clicked loudly on the bare floorboards. The floor was old, warped, and worm-eaten. In one spot the wood boards looked uneven and mismatched.

Something brushed against my fur, and I jumped. The empty room was starting to give me the creeps!

I began to edge my way toward the door. "Er . . . I love what's been done with the place. I'll have to take the complete tour later, just as soon as I check something downstairs."

I slowly made my move to get out of the room. At that very moment, the door, which had been partly open, slammed shut. For the first time since I arrived at the house, fear began to grab at the scruff of my neck.

"Snap out of it!" I told myself. "You're the great adventurer—start acting like one!" Bravely, I went over to the door and scratched with all my strength. But the door would not budge.

My feeling of uneasiness grew. The walls of the room seemed to close in tighter and tighter. A cold sweat broke out on my muzzle. Desperately, I looked around me. The window! I raced over to it, pawed at the shutters to open them, then looked out.

It opened on an empty courtyard at least a hundred feet below. There was no ledge to jump out onto. The damp outside walls of the house were as steep as a cliff. If I would try to escape through this window, I would surely fall to my doom on the cobblestones below.

I . . . think I may be in trouble here!

A choking feeling of panic swept over me. The longer I stayed in the room, the stronger my sense of horror grew. I wished that I could run out the door, out to the landing, down the stairs, and away from this miserable house. But I could not.

As I racked my brain for a way to escape, I suddenly noticed an awful noise. It sounded as though the walls were breathing in and out. With a sense of creeping horror, I felt cold breath on my paws. I looked down. A weird mist was seeping up through the cracks in the floorboards!

And that wasn't all. The floor began to glow with a strange light. Spooky green fingers of it drifted up through the floorboards like a ghostly hand.

I threw myself at the door. *Ugh! Must get out . . . must escape . . . must— What's that!*

Two glowing eyes burned out at me from the darkness. They looked like a cat's eyes, or a snake's. Whatever they belonged to, they were yellow, beady, and cold—and they seemed to pierce right through my fur!

Miserably, I rolled myself into a ball on the bare floor. I wondered who would find me, and when. Closing my eyes, I was gripped by a blast of arctic cold. . . .

Hey, it's really cold in here! Wishbone looked around the garage and shivered. A chilly breeze ruffled his fur.

Then he took a sniff. "The nose knows—an open window!"

Following the smell of fresh air, Wishbone jumped up on a bench at the side of the garage. Then he sniffed again.

Yesss! The side window is open a crack. Now, to make my escape!

Wishbone pushed his nose through the small opening. He tried one paw, then the other, and finally his whole head.

But it was no use. The opening was too small for him to fit through. And he couldn't open the window any farther.

Then Wishbone realized he was not alone. Something was watching him. Two glowing spots peered out of the darkness. . . .

"You looking at me?" Wishbone challenged the fiery eyes. "It's a terrible feeling, to be locked up as spooky eyes stare at you! Come to think of it, that's just how the young adventurer felt in 'The Haunters and the Haunted'. . . ."

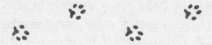

The cold and damp seeped through my hide, all the way from the tip of my nose to the end of my tail. My friend's words came back to haunt me: *You may live to regret this.*

Suddenly, I remembered my revolver.

My confidence returned. *Of course! Why didn't I think of it sooner?* I could aim out the window, into the courtyard. The sound of the shot would echo off the outer walls. As soon as someone heard the noise from the shot, help would come, and I'd be rescued!

I wagged my tail with relief. I reached a paw toward the revolver I carried. . . .

Both of my trusty weapons—the revolver and the dagger—were gone!

"Not funny," I barked. "That revolver cost me a month's allowance. May I have my weapons back, please?" I said into the darkness.

I turned around to see who—or what—might have taken them. And I saw something that made my blood run cold!

Out of the closed door, a shape began to form. It was that of a young man. He had long curly hair and a thin moustache. *Look how he's dressed! Those old-fashioned buckles and knee breeches have not been in style since Queen Elizabeth's time—and that was five whole monarchs ago.*

Then I noticed that the young man's skin was deathly pale. I realized I was looking at a real, honest-to-goodness ghost!

The ghost came toward me with slow, careful steps. His movements were scary and stiff. Then he stopped, and I wanted to howl in terror.

Piercing serpent's eyes glowed out of his ugly face. And they were aimed straight at me!

Suddenly, he raised his arm over his head. Just in time, I ducked. I heard the whistle of a dagger slice through the air.

Was it something I said? Hey! You're not kidding, are you! He kept coming at me. The dagger flew closer and closer to my throat. With a low howl, I turned my head away, expecting the worst.

Then I saw something that filled me with joy. Through the window the moon came out from behind patchy clouds. It shone silver, clear, and calm. A beam of light spilled into the room.

At once, the murderous-looking ghost vanished. The door that led to the landing swung open. I made my way slowly to the door. Lying in the doorway were two soggy pieces of parchment paper.

I picked them up in my mouth and ran from the room and almost galloped down the stairs. I felt as if I'd been given a new leash on life. There was the living room! There was my book! The crackling fire was music to my ears.

As I warmed myself by the hearth, my courage returned. I would win that hundred-pound bet. "It's going to take more than some pale-faced phantom to scare me away from this house!" I barked. *Okay, the*

dagger part was pretty convincing. But you're not getting rid of me that easily!

I was now certain of one thing—whatever was haunting the house and terrifying its residents, came from *that room!*

The night wore on. I turned to the two pieces of parchment paper I'd found on the floor upstairs.

I cocked my head as I studied them. *They're letters, and they date back fifty years! They seem to be written by a man and a woman. The letters seem to describe some terrible events that happened in this house. He's telling her not to breathe a word about them.*

"Why do I get the feeling she's not breathing *at all* anymore? But these letters are real evidence that something strange happened in this house. I'll show them to the owner and—"

I suddenly froze. The letters fell from my paws. From under a mahogany table, a woman's hand reached out. The flesh all over it was wrinkled and spotted with age.

But the hand was as real as my own paws! Slowly, ever so slowly, the hand reached out and felt its way toward me.

Er . . . looking for these?

The hand closed tightly over the letters.

Hey, sure—be my guest!

In an instant, the hand and letters disappeared under the table.

Before I had a chance to investigate, three loud knocks echoed throughout the house. I gasped in alarm, wondering if it was the ghost from upstairs, looking for his mail.

Then I realized the sound was coming from the front door.

Hey, someone want to get that? . . . Don't bother—I'm closer!

I hurried to answer it, glad for the excuse to leave the room. My old college roommate stood at the door. He was worried about my safety, he explained, and decided to check up on me. Then he leaned closer to study me in the dim light given off from the street-lamp near the house.

"Oh, my word!" he cried. "Are you all right? You're as pale as a ghost!"

Quickly, I told him what I had seen. He seemed visibly shaken. "The wager is off! Please, leave here at once. Nothing good can come from your staying here any longer."

But I was full of dogged determination to complete my mission. As stubborn as if I had a rope gripped between my teeth, I had given my promise to the house's owner. Nothing would make me drop it.

"Have no fear," I told my friend. "I *will* collect that hundred pounds and unlock the mystery of this house! And I know just where to start. . . ."

Have no fear. If there's a way out of this garage, I will find it!

Perched on the bench, Wishbone tried to ignore the two glowing spots in the corner. In the darkness, they looked like evil red eyes.

"There must be *some* way out of here. Maybe if I think very hard . . ."

Wishbone squeezed his eyes shut. The next second, the fur stood up on the terrier's back.

Something was *thumping* on the other side of the garage door. Something a *lot* bigger than a cat.

Well, I made something happen, all right. But it's not what the cute little dog was hoping for. In fact, it's a lot like Bulwer-Lytton's story. Just when the young adventurer thinks he is about to solve the mystery of the haunted house, he has another surprise waiting for him. . . .

I went back up the stairs to the small door near the landing.

As I entered the forbidding room, the same feeling of fear that I had before came over me.

I shook it off as best I could. I went straight to the boarded-up patch on the floor.

"This job calls for someone who has top-dog-digging talent. Who does that remind me of? I've got it—me!"

With determination, I dug in my nails. The boards were old and rotten. I quickly tore them away from the rest of the floor. Underneath was a trapdoor.

Hmm . . . large enough for a man to fit through. Or even a good-sized ghost? Ignoring my growing uneasiness, I tugged at the crumbling bolts with my teeth. Though they tasted terrible, they finally gave way, and I pushed the trapdoor aside.

Below me lay a hidden chamber.

Thin beams of moonlight shone into the dark opening. I peered down at the room. There was just enough light to see pieces of rotting furniture and an old-fashioned chest.

I wonder if the owner knows about this additional room. He should charge more rent. After gathering all my courage, I jumped down through the opening.

It was a lot farther down than it looked. I finally tumbled to the damp ground. Inside the chamber, a sense of clamminess and rot lay over everything. I scrambled to all fours. I found a moldy-looking candle, lit it, then opened the chest.

Inside I found old-fashioned clothes. They were richly decorated with lace and velvets. But the smell was worse than an army of wet cats! "I've seen better stuff at flea markets—including the fleas. No one has worn clothes like these in one hundred years!" I exclaimed, flinging them aside.

Underneath the clothes lay a small red book.

Did I say "book"? Why, there's only one page inside! I leaned forward to read it in the candlelight.

"This is in Latin. Good thing I studied that when I was in the university. But— Hey! This was not on the final!"

My hide stiffened as I read the words of doom aloud: "'Evil will fall on the walls of this house, and on all who live inside it. Abandon all hope, ye who enter here!'"

I think "ye" means me. . . . So I am . . . outta here!

I was about to jump up onto the edge of the chest, when I noticed something else in the chest. I dragged it out and held it up to the light.

It was a miniature portrait of a finely dressed nobleman. He had a long, narrow face. But those eyes! Snakelike, they stared out of the portrait, yellow, beady, and cold.

The colors of the picture look bright and new—but check out the date! It says 1750—that's more than a century old. . . . Hey, pal, you look pretty good for your age. Scary, but good.

That was when I heard it—the sound of a heavy object being pushed overhead. I looked up. . . . My fur stood on end!

Someone was standing above the trapdoor opening. It looked like a man. I could smell the mold rising from his splendid clothes, see the gleam of his yellow eyes, and hear his laughter . . . as the trapdoor began to creak closed over my head!

I leaped up, trying to escape from the chamber before I was sealed in. But my four paws slipped on the slimy, oozing walls of the small room. Cold panic swept through my body. In an instant, all hope for freedom would be gone. I would be buried alive,

with only a Latin curse and a spooky portrait to keep me company. . . .

Curse! Did I say "curse"?

Quickly, I grabbed the book of Latin in my mouth. As the trapdoor was about to slam shut, I ran to the candle and stuck the book right into the flame.

In an instant, the book shriveled to ashes. A deafening groan rocked the house. I dug my nails into the floor as the room swayed and the walls cracked.

Horrible screams filled the stale air. The dreadful noise seemed to last for hours. But when I looked up, moonlight poured into the chamber. The trapdoor was open.

My hunch had paid off! By destroying the book, I had lifted the curse. The evil spirit that had haunted the house for so many years was gone—and so was its human form, the man with the yellow eyes.

So long! I thought, as I leaped up on the chest and then scrambled out of the hole. *Don't forget to write! . . . On second thought, let's* not *stay in touch.*

That was the last I saw of the haunted house. I went to the owner and told him what I had seen.

When I mentioned the letters, Mr. J—— nodded. "I think I know who wrote them. Years ago, the lady who managed the house for me had married a scoundrel—a pirate, she said. On the same day that her brother was scheduled to inherit the family fortune, he was found dead in that room upstairs. The pirate disappeared, taking all the money with him."

"So the lady and her husband plotted together to kill her brother!"

Mr. J—— shook his head. "She told me that 'they' who haunted the house caused his death, and that 'they' would return for her!"

I fought off a shiver. "I think 'they' returned, all right—and never left!" I showed him the portrait. "Is this the pirate?"

The owner gasped. "Exactly as she described him. But . . . that painting is over a hundred years old!"

"So was the book I found, and the chest," I said.

"But how did all the objects get there?" he cried. "Who brought this ancient curse on my house?"

I paused and twitched my whiskers. "I'll try to answer that. Those objects were buried in your house many years ago. They belong to the nobleman who built the house. Since his death he has haunted the place. Sometimes he appears as a real-live person—like your manager's husband, the pirate—and sometimes as a ghost. This evil spirit has tried to destroy everyone in his path. If I can make a suggestion, it's time you threw him out—for good!"

On my advice, Mr. J—— had the room and its secret chamber torn down. Together we burned the small portrait. Finally, the curse was lifted!

I met my old college friend at the Cosmopolitan Club the next day. I was there to collect my reward. I treated him to a fine meal, after which he made a toast. "Here's to your next great adventure! And this time I'll double the bet!"

I pretended not to hear him.

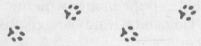

Wishbone sat on the cold garage floor, thinking about the haunted-house story. Something *thumped* again on the garage door. Wishbone swallowed hard. *I am a brave hunter in the night—I will face this thing!*

At that moment, the moon peeked out from behind a cloud. It shone on something at Wishbone's feet.

Hey, look! It's the Barneses' remote control.

Wishbone stepped on the red button. Two glowing spots in the corner began to blink. The fiery red eyes were back. With a loud squeak, the garage door lifted up. In the moonlight, Wishbone saw that the red eyes belonged to the automatic garage door opener.

"Hey, thanks," he said, as he rushed outside—and leaped over a large branch that had blown against the garage. A cold wind swept the branch away, and the garage door began to go back down. "This wind is making everything go haywire."

Something brushed against Wishbone's fur. A pair of yellow eyes gleamed out of the darkness.

Wishbone barked! "I have you now!"

The shape sped off into the night, down Forest Lane.

Wishbone followed right behind!

Tails of Terror

4

"A Brush with Terror"

by Nancy Holder

Inspired by "The Portrait-Painter's Story"
by Charles Dickens

Illustrated by Jane McCreary

Now, where is that black cat? Wishbone wondered. He had chased the feline through Forest Lane. Wishbone had lost track of the cat at the post office on Oak Street. The white-with-brown-and-black-spots Jack Russell terrier trotted over a carpet of crackling autumn leaves along the street. *I'm sure he ran this way. I know every inch of this street like the back of my paws . . . all four of them.*

But this Halloween night, nothing looked the same. Everything was creepy. The moon, looking like a big, glowing jack-o'-lantern, grinned down from the dark night sky. Silvery moonbeams cast spooky shadows across the windows of stores. Bare tree branches stretched out like eerie skeleton arms, waving in the wind.

Wishbone heard a noise. *Could be the cat.* Sure enough, his keen nose caught the familiar smell of tuna breath! *Blech! Getting warmer,* he told himself, as he got down and crawled on his stomach. He made his way slowly through the leaves to a streetlamp. He jumped up and placed his front paws on the foot of the lamp. He stretched up tall. *No cat.*

Wishbone dropped back to all fours on the sidewalk. He moved on with his nose planted very closely to the ground. All the better to sniff for clues. Fog swirled around him as the wind began to blow. The white vapor rolled and spun like smoke. It was hard to see, but the terrier's sharp sense of smell gave him all the direction he needed.

Before he knew it, he had passed Rosie's Rendezvous Books & Gifts. Oakdale Sports & Games was up ahead. The lights in both buildings were off. Halloween decorations fluttered in the brisk wind. There was not another soul on Oak Street. He was all alone. On Halloween night.

Look! In the distance, near a streetlamp, Wishbone saw something move in front of Oakdale Sports & Games.

The shape was glowing! Wishbone barked in surprise. Then, just as he neared the entrance of the store, the shape vanished!

Excuse me? He inspected the door and windows, which were decorated for Halloween. *How could it just disappear?*

And if it wasn't a cat, what was it? Let's see . . . Halloween . . . not a cat . . . something that can just vanish . . .

The fur rose along Wishbone's spine. A chill shot through his hide. *Maybe it was a ghost!*

A ghost, appearing and disappearing on a chilly, foggy night . . . That reminds me of a very scary tale called "The Portrait-Painter's Story."

"The Portrait-Painter's Story" was written by the famous English author Charles Dickens. He lived from 1812 to 1870. He wrote many kinds of stories, and he is well known for his ghostly tales.

This story was first published by Dickens in 1861, in a magazine he produced, called *All Year Round*.

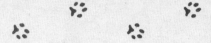

Gazing at a cardboard goblin on the door, Wishbone imagined he was in London in 1858. *He* was the famous portrait painter. And he was about to have a strange adventure. . . .

I will never forget what happened to me in the year 1858. Of course, no one who has seen a ghost would forget about it! But I am an artist. I have learned to take notice of things that other people do not see. I can still see every terrifying detail clearly, as if I had painted every scene.

It was a horrid day for travel. October in London is always cold and rainy. Though it was barely noon, the sky was black with storm clouds. Arched stone buildings and brick warehouses were dull and colorless. Men in dark capes and frock coats hurried to their jobs. The bell-shaped woolen skirts of the ladies swayed in the strong wind. Old newspapers and pieces of trash whipped down narrow, shadowed alleys.

To stay warm, I wore a heavy black overcoat and a top hat. But as I boarded the London train heading for the countryside, the icy rain still soaked through my clothes all the way to my hide. My half-frozen paws slid on the wet wooden floorboards of the train. I wished with all my heart that I could stay home. Oh, what I would have given for a nice, soft chair, a good book, and some meaty beef ribs!

But my train ride was only the beginning of a long journey. A rich family had hired me to paint their portrait. I would travel the rest of the day to get to their home. *At least we'll have dinner when I arrive. Hopefully, they will serve something nice and hot! And lots of it!*

In the train, I hopped onto my red-velvet seat and circled twice before lying down. The train began to move. The sound of its engine—a steady *chug, chug, chug*—was like a heartbeat. Outside, thunder rumbled and lightning crackled. I was glad to be out of the bad weather and on my way.

Soon the train left the city behind. Pressing my black nose against the window, I could see nothing except heavy, gray rain. It was not a fit day outside for man or beast.

I was about to sink my teeth into the daily newspaper when I noticed that I was not alone. *How curious,* I thought, folding up my paper with my muzzle. I placed it between my forepaws. *No one was here before, and I heard no one sit down.*

I hope whoever it is brought snacks.

Across from me sat a pale young lady. She had not been there two seconds before. Her skin was as white as a thick London fog. She was dressed all in black. When she saw me looking at her, she smiled a very happy smile.

"Ah. There you are," she said. "And how are you today?"

I was puzzled by her friendly tone. My left ear

flapped over as I cocked my head. *Do I know her? Have we met before?*

I did not want to appear rude, but I did not remember her. I answered, "It is nice to see you."

"It is nice to see me," she echoed strangely. Her face became serious. "It is good that you *can* see me."

"Ah . . ." I said. *What does she mean by that?* I did not know how to answer.

"Tell me, how is your business?" she asked. "It's wonderful that you are so busy with work. But of course, you are an excellent artist. Everyone wants you to paint their picture."

I was even more confused. *Has she posed for me? Have I painted her picture?*

"Thank you," I answered. I am a modest sort of breed, and so I changed the subject. Folding my paws politely, I said, "Will you travel far today?"

Her eyes were large and dark. "You cannot imagine how far I have traveled already." Her voice was very soft. "I have come a very long way."

"Then you must be tired," I said. My fur rose slightly along my neck. My tail stiffened just a little bit. I felt uneasy and a little nervous in her company. *It's simply that I can't recall who she is,* I told myself.

But there was something else about her that gave me something to chew on. As the train chugged along, I watched her reflection against the dark window. The young lady's white face seemed to float in the darkness. I tried to speak in a pleasant way to her, but I often ran out of things to say. Right in front of my big brown eyes, she seemed to fade away. Then, when I blinked, she would be there, smiling at me.

In truth, I was relieved when the train pulled into the next station. It was my stop. From there, I had to change to another train. I explained this to her.

"It has been nice speaking with you," I said. I gave her a parting wag of my tail as I prepared to hop off my seat.

Her smile was very odd. "Oh, we shall see each other again," she said. Then she leaned forward and held out her hand. I took it in my paw. Her skin was freezing-cold.

Whoa! This is weird. . . . And I am outta here!

My nails clacked on the wooden floor as I left the train. She remained behind, staring at me through the window we had shared.

Who is she? How does she know me? . . .

Those questions still haunted me as I rode on the second train. Then I hired a private horse-drawn carriage to drive through the terrible storm.

At nightfall, I finally arrived at the beautiful home where I was expected. A servant showed me upstairs to my room. He explained to me that because of the weather, the family had been delayed. I was to dress for dinner and then warm myself by the fire downstairs.

I did so. Carefully, I opened my traveling bag with my teeth and pulled out my formal evening clothes. In the mirror, I made sure my collar was on straight. *Hey, I'm one handsome animal,* I thought with satisfaction.

Then I trotted down the stairs.

When I entered the room where the fire burned brightly, a figure all in black stood warming its hands. The face was turned away from me. As my paws clicked on the hardwood floor, the figure turned and faced me.

It was the young lady from the first train! I could not stop the yip of surprise that escaped my throat.

"I told you that we would see each other again," she told me.

I was amazed. However, I did not yip a second

time. I bowed my muzzle almost to the floor, and she curtsied.

"How did you travel here?" I asked. "The second train I took was the last one for the night!"

The young lady's voice was low. "I did not come here by train."

"In what way, then?"

"Sorrow brought me here," she said. "Sorrow of the worst kind."

Her face was very white, her eyes very dark. As she stood there, I felt there was something unnatural about her. I believed that my artist's mind was taking in details that my normal thinking could not. My fur bristled. I was suddenly terrified. I did not know exactly why. I had to stop myself from growling at her.

At that very moment, the servant appeared at the doorway of the room. He bowed to me and said, "Sir, the family has arrived. They await you at dinner."

I noted that he did not speak to the woman in black. I thought that was not polite. But it was not my business to correct him.

The servant showed us the way to the dining room. We walked down a hallway. My sharp hearing picked up the rustle of the woman's skirts as she followed behind me. Once I glanced over my shoulder to look at her—and I saw nothing! But still I heard her skirts! Then I blinked, and she was there once more.

The light in here is playing tricks on me, I thought. *This hallway is dark, and I cannot see very well.*

103

I'm spooking myself, Wishbone decided. *The foggy moonlight is making me think I'm seeing things that aren't really there.*

He perked his ears forward and sniffed along the bottom of the door at the sporting-goods store. He neither saw nor heard anything strange. *This adventure's over,* he decided. *It's late. And I'm hungry. Maybe Ellen forgot to put away our trick-or-treat candy. I'm ready for a pre-bedtime snack.*

Wishbone turned to go.

Something flashed in front of the sporting-goods store. The glowing object was back. Through the thick fog, it rippled and suddenly grew larger. *It has a face.* Big, angry-looking black eyes glared at him. Its mouth stretched into an evil grin across its face.

Wishbone took two steps back and barked.

The creature came closer.

At dinner, I was to sit in the chair directly across the table from the strange young lady in black. We were almost as close once more as we had been on the train. To my surprise, the only other people who came to dinner were my host and hostess. The rest of the family was not present. As I hopped onto my seat, I waited to be introduced to the pale woman. But my employer and his wife completely ignored their other guest.

Perhaps she is a governess, here to care for the couple's children, I thought, as the butler placed a bowl of warm soup in front of me. Such ladies were often invited to dine with the family, but they were not treated like upper-class purebreds.

I bent my head and joyfully lapped up my soup. I was careful not to dip my nose into the tasty broth.

"How delicious," I said to the lady in black. I licked my chops. "Do you find it so?"

"Thank you," my hostess replied. I realized she thought I had spoken to her.

"You're very welcome," I answered.

I picked up my napkin and wiped stray drops of soup from my muzzle and whiskers.

Then I spoke again to the lady in black. "Would you please pass me the pepper?"

"It would be my pleasure," said my host. He reached directly in front of the pale woman and placed the silver pepper shaker in front of me.

This is odd, I thought, as I sprinkled pepper into my soup. *Both the husband and his wife act as if the young lady is not here.*

Stranger still was what happened after dinner. News of my presence had spread throughout the town. The family's friends and neighbors were curious to meet me. Soon I was very busy making small-talk with a roomful of guests. I spoke so much that my mouth went dry and my tail began to droop.

All this time, the pale young woman watched me. She spoke to no one, and no one spoke to her. The woman remained a mystery. Even in the room full of people, she seemed alone.

After all the guests had met me, I was free to wander through the large dining room. There was a chill,

which others had spoken of. I warmed my fur by the fire. I got so close that I nearly burned my tail.

I had an odd feeling that someone was standing behind me. I turned around. The chill returned. The lady in black smiled at me. But her dark eyes were sad.

"Is there something I might fetch for you?" I asked her, bowing over my front paws. "Or is there some other service I may do for you?"

"Indeed, there is." She took a deep breath, as if to gather courage. "I would be forever grateful if you would paint my portrait."

I did not understand why she was shy to ask me. Several people at the party had already made the same request.

"It is how I make my living," I answered. "I would be most happy to paint you." To prove my point, I thumped my slightly toasted tail. *Ouch!*

"Ah." She was greatly relieved. "That is wonderful. It will make all the difference."

All the difference? I wondered. *All the difference in what? What does she mean by that?* I did not want to seem rude by asking, so I kept my questions to myself.

"Would you like to pose for the picture in London?" I asked her. "Or shall I trot on over to your house?" I asked her.

This question clearly upset her. "I cannot pose for the portrait," she said. "You must draw me from memory."

I cocked my head. "Alas," I told her. "I do not think I would be able to do that. I will need to see you many times to do a good job."

This pained her greatly. "I cannot do that," she insisted. "Wait." She opened her handbag and pulled out a drawing, which had been torn from a book. "This is a portrait of a famous lady. I have often been told I look like her."

She placed the picture between my teeth. Carefully, I laid it on the floor and inspected it. I studied it so hard I almost dampened it with the end of my nose.

"Close, but no cigar," I told her.

"I beg your pardon?" she asked.

I did not want to lie. "I don't think you look like her very much at all," I said.

"Oh." She sighed. "So it will not help you to have the picture?"

I shook my head. She seemed to take the news badly. "Perhaps it would help a little." I wagged my tail in a friendly manner. "And I suppose I could try to paint you from memory."

"Oh, thank you so much!" she said gratefully. She clenched her fists and stared at me. "You cannot know how important this is!"

I was a bit startled, so I backed up a few steps.

Then from behind me, my hostess said, "Oh *there* you are! I'm so sorry that my friends have been bothering you!"

I turned to face her. I forced myself to sound calm and pleasant. "Not at all," I told her. "They're all very nice. And I have had a lovely chat with this nice young woman."

My hostess raised her eyebrows. She asked, "Which nice young woman?"

"Why, this one." I turned to introduce them to each other at last.

But the pale young lady in black had vanished!

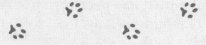

The demon face of the glowing creature pushed through the swirling fog. The eyes were deep holes against the eerie white glow of its face. Wishbone's fur stood on end. His heartbeat hammered.

I think I'll pick up the trail of that black cat, he reminded himself.

He thought he caught a whiff of the cat. He whirled around toward the street and started to run. Then—*crack!* A large wooden sign fell over in the wind. It blocked his path.

Okay, I'll take a detour. He whirled back around.

While the terrier's back was turned, the ghostly creature had come closer.

Wishbone moved forward and to the left to avoid the creature. But the creature followed his every move. Then it rushed at him. Wishbone backed up, and he bumped right into the door of Oakdale Sports & Games.

Now the thing was almost on top of him. . . .

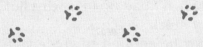

The pale young lady was gone. I asked the other guests if anyone had seen her leave. They asked me who I was talking about. No one remembered seeing such a woman at all. I asked the butler about her, but he claimed he never saw her, either.

"We had dinner with her," I reminded him. "Your master and mistress and I. We were four all together."

"I do beg your pardon, sir," he said. "But truly, there were only the three of you. My master, my mistress, and yourself, as you say."

Then why wasn't there enough dessert for me to have a second helping? I wanted to ask. Suddenly a chill came over me. Could it be true that no one else had seen the young lady?

I did not speak of her again. I painted the family's portrait. They were most pleased. Then soon after that, I returned to London.

After a time I forgot about the young lady. I had many pictures to paint, and I stayed very busy.

Then one day, as twilight fell, I saw her in my artist's studio. I was startled. She had not rung the bell, and my door was locked. But she stood before me, looking quite worried.

"Have you painted my picture?" she asked.

I confessed that I had not. "I really need to have you pose for the painting," I told her. "I cannot do it from memory."

I invited her to sit down and took out a sketch-book. It was clear to me that she did not want me to look closely at her. I had no idea why. But I was able to draw two very quick sketches.

"Will they be enough to guide you?" she asked.

"I hope so," I told her honestly.

She stood up and shook my hand firmly. "Then, good-bye," she said.

I showed her to the door. As I stood in the gloom of early evening, I watched her go down the steps to the sidewalk in front of my studio. Before her shoes had touched the bottom step, she had melted into the gray twilight.

Shivering, I closed the door with my muzzle.

Soon after, I had to take some of my paintings to another part of England. I packed them up and took them to the railway station a week before I was to leave. As was the custom of the time, packages went on one train, and people on another.

At last I left on my trip. But when I arrived at my stop, the railway clerk discovered that someone had taken my paintings and put them on another train! They were now waiting for me in a small village.

When I asked who had done this, he explained that no one had seen anybody near the baggage train.

"It must have been a ghost who moved your things," he joked.

To me, this remark was not funny. I was supposed to deliver those paintings to another city. Rather than wait for their return, I traveled to the small village to get them.

It was a long train ride, made more difficult because of the cold weather. Even with my heavy black overcoat, I could not keep warm. My only comfort was a sweet biscuit and some hot tea.

I chewed and sipped. I thought of the train trip when I first had met the pale young woman. *So many strange things have happened since that day.*

Placing one chilled paw after another, I left the train and stood on the platform. I placed my traveling bag beside me. It was very late. There was no one there to help me with my problem. I would have to return in the morning, when the station's office was open.

I was about to walk through the chilly rain to the local inn. Suddenly, an older gentleman raced up to me. He was quite out of breath. He bent down and took my paw, shaking it very hard.

"Thank heaven you have come!" he cried. "Now you can rescue me from my misery!" He raised his hands in frustration. "Now they will see that I am not insane!"

"Sir," I said, pawing at the space between us. I also barked—quietly—to get his attention. But the man was not listening.

"My daughter sent you," he went on. "From the grave, she guided you here."

Hoo-boy! I thought. *This is getting really strange.*

He led me to his carriage. Lightning cracked and flashed above us in the heavy rain. The carriage wheels dragged through the thick mud. The horses whinnied and stamped. They were afraid.

I knew the feeling. I huddled inside the compartment and listened to my teeth chatter.

Soon after we got going, the man told me he had a daughter, Caroline.

"I loved her more than anything on this Earth," he said. "But my daughter died suddenly. It happened four months ago."

I was on a train four months ago, I thought. A shiver shot down my furred spine.

"I think about her day and night," he went on to say. "I cannot rest. I cannot eat. I have no picture of her, and I fear I will forget what she looked like. I cannot imagine anything worse than to forget my daughter!"

He grabbed my shoulders. "You are here to paint her portrait for me!"

"Excuse me?" I yipped.

He wasn't finished. "I go into a deep trance, and I see her there before me. Three times this has happened to me. Each time, she was with *you!* The first time was on a train. The second time, it was at a party. And the third time, I saw her at an artist's studio."

"My studio!" I asked in shock.

"And then, tonight, I had another vision. I saw you clearly on the train. I knew you were coming to our village. I believe this is a sign that you are here to paint her portrait."

I nodded slowly. He had me on that one. "Tell me, sir, what did your daughter look like?"

He tried to tell me. However, like many people who are not artists, he couldn't give me the details to make his description clear. Then he said, "I have a book at home. It contained a portrait of a woman who

113

looked very much like my daughter. But, sadly, some-one ripped the picture out of the book!"

I jumped down from my seat in the carriage and opened my travel bag with my teeth. With trembling paws, I searched through my belongings. I found the picture the pale young woman had given me. I pulled it out and showed it to the elderly man.

"This is the very picture!" he cried. "Oh, sir, my daughter has been with you!"

I was unable to speak for several moments. *I have been haunted,* I thought. *The ghost of this man's daughter came back from the grave. I promised a dead woman that I would paint her portrait!*

"I shall honor her request," I finally managed to say to the elderly man. I got back on the seat.

"Oh, thank you, sir! Thank you a million times!" he said, pumping my paw.

Then he hugged me.

In the window of the carriage, I saw the image of the pale young woman. For a moment, her eyes locked on mine. Lightning flashed, and I studied her features—lips, nose, eyes.

I nodded at her. It was my way of telling her that her picture would be a masterpiece.

She nodded back.

After that, her image faded away.

I went to her father's house and immediately began to paint. Though I did not see her again, her face still haunted me. I worked all night to get her image just right.

At dawn, the old man came from his bedroom to see the portrait. "It is my sweet girl!" he cried. "My darling, dead Caroline!"

Caroline's face still haunts me. Her likeness has made me famous all over the world. Everyone always says her portrait is so lifelike.

If only they knew.

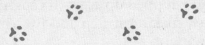

Wishbone barked at the phantom as it rushed toward him. His back side pressed against the door. There was no escape. The round, black eyes stared fiercely at him. The mouth shot open in a wicked, silent laugh.

Then it landed right on top of him!

Save yourself! Wishbone cried silently.

He bit at the phantom, rolling over and over as he fought to free himself. He got a piece of it in his mouth. It ripped!

He knew that taste. *Blech! It's plastic!*

The thing lay limp as he crawled out from under it. With his paw, he nudged his fallen enemy.

It's a Halloween mask!

It was nothing but a thin sheet of plastic with scary cut-out eyes and a jagged-shaped mouth. It had been attached to the roof of Oakdale Sports & Games with a string. The string had come loose. The wind had made the plastic ripple and float.

"Hah!" Wishbone sat on his haunches. He scratched himself behind the ear with his left hind leg. "I knew that's what it was all along!"

The terrier calmed down. His heart no longer pounded.

"So is *this* the end of my Halloween adventure? Maybe I'll just let the black cat have the rest of the night off."

Leaving the mask behind, Wishbone began to trot toward home.

The wind whipped up again. It caught the ghostly face on a gust, making it flap and fly. Then it soared away into the night.

In the distance, Wishbone heard an owl hoot.

Or was it ghostly laughter?

Tails of Terror

5

"Fearful Fetch"

by B. B. Calhoun

Inspired by "Wandering Willie's Tale"
by Sir Walter Scott

Illustrated by Don Punchatz

After wrestling with the Halloween mask in front of Oakdale Sports & Games, Wishbone continued down Oak Street. He came to a stop near Rosie's Rendezvous Books & Gifts. He sniffed, searching for the scent of the black cat. But the air was filled with the ripe smell of pumpkins.

Suddenly he saw it—a flash of the cat's black tail! It probably was headed toward Jackson Park. Wishbone took off down the street after it.

"You won't escape this time!" he called after the cat. The chase had been going on for quite a while.

As Wishbone entered Jackson Park, the moon was full, and the trees cast long shadows across the grass. Even the familiar T-ball field looked scary in that light.

Wishbone glanced quickly from side to side, his ears alert for danger. He shook off a shiver. No sign of the cat.

There is nothing at all to be afraid of, he told himself. *After all, this is the park, a place for— Aaah! What's that?*

Wishbone spotted a flash of something white underneath some nearby bleacher seats. He moved to investigate.

Suddenly, he realized what it was.

"A soccer ball!" he said happily. He sniffed the object. It had a very familiar smell. "*My* soccer ball! Hey, how did you get here?" Thrilled with his discovery, he pounced on the ball.

With the ball in his mouth, Wishbone looked around quickly. There were long, creepy shadows stretched across the grass. *How did my soccer ball get here by itself, anyway?* Suddenly, he was eager to get out of there.

Wishbone made his way off the field. He trotted into the wooded part of the park. Something about this spooky situation seemed familiar. . . . A hero braving a frightening journey to get back something that belonged to him . . . Why, of course! It was Sir Walter Scott's scary short story "Wandering Willie's Tale."

Sir Walter Scott was a Scottish writer who lived from 1771 to 1832. He wrote poetry, novels, and even history books! Many of his stories, including "Wandering Willie's Tale," take place in the Scottish Highlands.

The story is set in the 1600s, on the estate of Sir Robert Redgauntlet. He was a powerful nobleman, a landowner, and a man greatly feared for his terrible temper.

As Wishbone remembered the story, he imagined *he* was brave young Steenie Steenson. He rented land on Sir Robert's property. He was a top-dog bagpipe player, but he was not very good at taking care of his money. Like the others who lived on Sir

Robert's land, he was supposed to pay his rent every six months to the nobleman in the castle. But somehow, Steenie found himself two terms, a full year, behind in his rent to Sir Robert. . . .

Steenie Steenson trotted over the beautiful green hills of the Scottish Highlands. The cool morning mist was burning off as the sun rose higher in the sky. Steenie was headed toward Redgauntlet Castle. He knew Sir Robert was expecting him. He was moving as fast as his four legs would carry him. Sir Robert was top dog, or lord of the manor. Steenie knew he was really in the doghouse for being late—again—with his rent money.

Steenie's plaid kilt flew out behind him in the breeze as he ran. Without his bagpipes to weigh him down, Steenie was making good time. The fur pouch he wore around his belly bumped against his hind legs. Today Steenie's pouch held a cloth bag. It was filled with silver coins that jingled as Steenie ran.

Well, it wasn't exactly easy, but I finally came up with the rent money, Steenie told himself. Early that morning, Steenie had trotted around to Sir Robert's twenty other tenants. Most were happy to loan him money. He had been forced to beg to a few others. But at last Steenie had managed to scrape together what he owed his landlord.

After all, Steenie had thought, *shouldn't friends help ye out when yer in a tight spot?* Lucky for Steenie, he had always made friends easily.

Steenie knew that even Sir Robert had a bit of a

soft spot for him. The master of the estate had often asked Steenie in the past to play his bagpipes to entertain guests at the castle. Still, Steenie realized that it wasn't a good idea to get on the bad side of the master.

He's one guy whose bite is just as bad as—maybe even worse than—his bark. But now, at last, I can face Sir Robert with a heavy purse and a light heart.

Steenie ran up the stone path that led to the castle. He stared up at its huge, dark gray stone towers and turrets. A heavy wooden door stood before him. Steenie reached for the fringed bell-pull with his teeth. He gave the thick rope a healthy tug. Bells echoed inside the castle's thick stone walls.

A few moments later, Sir Robert's butler, Dugal MacCallum, answered the door. MacCallum had gray hair and a full gray beard. He wore a plaid kilt and a short jacket of dark green wool.

MacCallum's wrinkled face broke into a smile when he saw Steenie. "Ah, Steenie, at last!" He patted Steenie affectionately on the head. Then he lowered his voice. "The master has been asking for ye since early morning. But I'm afraid he isn't too well now. When ye didn't show up first thing, he got so upset that he had an attack of the gout."

Steenie nodded. He knew that Sir Robert was often troubled by gout, an illness of the joints that made his feet ache. "Sir Robert ought to get out more," Steenie said. "Run around. Chase a few butterflies."

MacCallum gave him a stern look.

"I know, I know," Steenie said with a little sigh. "No tenant should dare to tell the master what to do." With a shrug, he pulled the bag of coins out of his pouch with his mouth. "Well, thith silver outh to sheer him up," he said with the cloth bag in his teeth.

With a nod, MacCallum led Steenie into the castle. The two walked through a maze of huge, dark hallways. Candles flickered in their iron holders on all the walls. The pair headed up the stone stairs to a grand oak-paneled parlor.

Sir Robert was sitting in a huge armchair. He was a heavyset man, dressed in an enormous black velvet robe. His sore feet were propped up in front of him on a cushioned stool. On his lap he held the big rent book. It had a black-leather cover and brass closures.

Steenie put down his money bag. Sir Robert looked terrible. His face was ash-white. He had large, dark rings under the eyes.

Of course, Steenie realized, *my own face is white, and I have a ring around one eye, too. But that's different. On me it looks good.*

On Sir Robert's right side sat his pet monkey, named Major Weir. The monkey was one of the ugliest creatures Steenie had ever seen . . . or smelled.

Steenie's nostrils twitched. *Phew, buddy! I mean, I hate a bath as much as the next guy, but there's a limit. . . .*

"Steenie Steenson the piper!" Sir Robert said in a booming voice. He gave Steenie a fierce look. "Have ye come empty-handed? Because, if ye have—"

"Me? Of course not!" Steenie trotted forward with the bag of silver. "There ye go! Nothing to worry about! It's all there—every last coin." He put the bag in Sir Robert's lap, then sat back, his tail wagging.

Sir Robert opened the bag quickly. He smiled at

the sight of the shiny coins. "MacCallum," he told the butler, "take Steenie the piper downstairs for a cup of brandy. Have him wait while I count the silver and write the receipt."

MacCallum nodded.

Steenie turned to follow the butler. "Brandy, huh? Hey, MacCallum, do ye think I could have a snack with that? Some nice juicy sausages would be good, or maybe a nice piece of—"

Suddenly, Sir Robert let out a terrible yell. "Aaaaaaaah-yaaaa!"

Steenie stopped in his tracks. He whipped his head around.

Sir Robert waved his hands wildly in the air. His face was beet-red. He yelled again. His screams sounded worse than a broken bagpipe.

Steenie looked at Sir Robert in alarm. "Uh . . . okay, if ye feel that way about it, I guess I can skip the snack."

Sir Robert screamed again. "Aaaaaah! Aaaaaa-yaaaaaaa! Help me!"

MacCallum ran back to his master.

Sir Robert continued to yell.

Steenie took a careful step forward. "Excuse me, would it be better if I came back some other time to pick up my receipt?"

His voice was drowned out by more terrifying screams from Sir Robert. Before long, Major Weir began to scream, too. Then he got off the seat and ran around the room.

Servants rushed into the parlor from other parts of the castle. Steenie sat back on his haunches.

"Water! I need cool water for my burning feet!" Sir Robert was yelling.

Immediately, a servant rushed to get a bucket of water.

Steenie watched as Sir Robert dipped his feet down into the cold liquid. But as soon as his feet touched the water, he let out a horrible yell. "Aaaah! It's burning me!"

Wow! These rich guys sure are picky, Steenie thought. But then he noticed something amazing. He stared in wide-eyed surprise. Sure enough, the bucket bubbled over like an iron caldron when the water touched Sir Robert's flesh.

"Aaaaah! Wine! Wine!" Sir Robert bellowed. "I need wine to soothe my throat!"

MacCallum ran from the room. Soon he returned with a silver cup. He quickly handed it to his master. Sir Robert got ready to taste the wine.

Steenie watched with caution. "Uh . . . I don't know if that's such a good idea," he said. "I mean, ye might want to blow on that a little fir——"

Sir Robert let out another yell. He threw the cup at MacCallum. It bounced off the butler's head and landed not far from Steenie. A red stain spread on the carpet.

"Aaaaaaah-yaaaaa! That's not wine—it's blood!" Sir Robert cried. "What are ye trying to do to me?"

Blood? Steenie's round brown eyes opened wide. Carefully, he stepped forward. He sniffed at the red stain on the carpet in front of him. The fur on his back stood on end as he smelled the scent. *It is blood! The wine must have turned to blood when it touched Sir Robert's lips! What is going on here?*

Then Sir Robert let out the loudest, most horrifying scream of all. "Aaaa-aayaaaaaaa-*yaaaaaaa!*"

Steenie buried his face in the carpet. He covered his sensitive ears with his paws.

A moment later, the room fell silent. Just as suddenly as Sir Robert's screams had begun, they ended.

Steenie peeked out from between his paws. Sir Robert was slumped in his chair, motionless. He looked like a huge mountain of velvet.

Steenie sniffed the air. A strange, unearthly odor—stronger even than the smell of monkey—had filled the room.

MacCallum bent down beside his master. A moment later, he faced Steenie and the others in the room. His voice shook. "He's dead. The master is dead."

Steenie felt a shiver go through him from nose to tail. He trembled as Major Weir began to run wildly in circles around Sir Robert.

Suddenly, the monkey raced over to Steenie. It stared straight at him, then let out a few blood-curdling shrieks.

Steenie didn't hesitate another moment. "Okay, that's it! I am outta here!"

As quickly as he could, Steenie turned and ran from the room. He raced down the hall, his nails clicking and sliding on the smooth stone floor. Skidding around a corner, he headed straight for the stairs.

On the main floor of the castle, Steenie ran for the front door. He could still hear the terrible screams of Major Weir echoing through the castle behind him as he got outside.

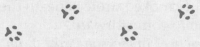

Wishbone made his way through the trees, the soccer ball still in his mouth. The wind began to pick up. Leaves swirled around him.

The shadows of trees moved threateningly across the grass. Wishbone looked right and then left, his ears alert for danger. Suddenly, the wooded area looked less familiar.

Why is this place looking strange to me? Wishbone thought in alarm. *Still, I have to keep going. The brave canine must never give up his daring rescue of the helpless . . . uh . . . soccer ball.*

He could hear the wind moaning. Soon the

moaning turned into a loud howling. Wishbone moved faster than ever.

Suddenly, Wishbone found himself in complete darkness. He tripped over something—a rotting log. He lost his balance. The ball flew from the grip of his teeth. It sailed through the air. He heard it bounce a few times, and then it disappeared.

"Hey? Where did it go?" Wishbone got up and trotted carefully in the direction that the ball had flown.

He came to the edge of a steep hill. He glanced down. There was his ball. It had landed in deep shadows near the bottom of a tree.

Wishbone eyed the tree. It was huge, with a twisted trunk. It towered over him.

And what's that in the trunk? It looks like . . . a face!

Sure enough, two dark black hollows glared at Wishbone. The crooked smile beneath them seemed to be daring him to come forward.

A haunted tree? In Jackson Park? It can't be . . . or can it? After all, it is Halloween . . . and a lot of strange things have already happened tonight.

Just then, Wishbone heard a deep groan. The fur along his back stood on end.

"Excuse me?" he said to the tree. "Did you say something?"

The tree's branches shook. They seemed to reach out toward him like long arms.

I know trees, and this is not the way they usually be-have, Wishbone thought. Meanwhile, the ball sat in the shadows at its roots.

The Jack Russell terrier remembered Redgauntlet

Castle. A lot of other creepy things had begun to happen there, as well. . . .

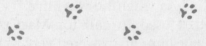

Several days after Sir Robert's death, Steenie received a message from Redgauntlet Castle. Sir Robert's son, Sir John, wanted to see the bagpipe player. Sir John was the new lord of the castle. He had inherited all that his father, Sir Robert, had owned. Steenie knew he had to come when he was called.

I wonder what Sir John wants, Steenie thought, as he got up on his horse. He took the reins in his teeth and trotted off. Then his ears pricked up with an exciting thought. *Maybe the old guy left me a little something in his will. After all, Sir Robert was always fond of me.* He rode his horse over the lush green hills, toward the castle. *Well, I'll soon know why I'm wanted at the castle.*

Steenie tied his horse to one of the iron bars of the castle gate. Then he headed up the stone path. At the door, he took the thick rope in his teeth and tugged on it to ring the bell.

The enormous door opened. To Steenie's surprise, a young red-haired maid stood in front of him. Sir Robert's old butler was nowhere in sight.

Steenie cocked his head. "Why, you're not Dugal MacCallum!"

The girl looked frightened. When she spoke, her voice trembled. "MacCallum was found dead. He had become ill after Sir Robert's death. He told us he was hearing the master blow on his silver whistle every night. He was haunted by the sound, especially since the master was dead." She lowered her voice to a near-whisper. "It was the very same way Sir Robert used to call for MacCallum when he was alive."

"Sir Robert used to call for MacCallum with a whistle?" Steenie himself answered very well to whistles. But he had no idea that the old butler did, too.

"Only at night," the maid replied. "The master used to whistle for MacCallum from his bed. He needed MacCallum to help him turn over. After the master died, his coffin was placed in his bedroom. MacCallum said his whistle continued to sound each night."

Poor MacCallum, Steenie thought. *He must have been absolutely terrified when he thought that he heard his master's whistle.*

The girl nearly whispered as she said, "They found MacCallum's body at the side of his master's coffin." She shook her head. "Ye would be better off not to enter this terrible place."

"Well, that may be true. But I've been called for—by the new master himself."

Steenie stepped inside the gloomy castle. The girl led him through the great, dark halls. As the click of his nails echoed through the stone hallways, Steenie tried to shake off a feeling of dread. *Whatever has been going on in Redgauntlet Castle lately gives me the creeps. I want absolutely no part of it. Too many people have been dropping like fleas.* But Steenie knew that he had to be at the castle. Sir John was the master there now. *Whatever Sir John commands—"come," "sit," "stay," "pay"—I have to obey what he says.*

The maid showed Steenie into the upstairs parlor. Steenie felt a shiver shoot from his nose to his tail as he recognized the room. *It was here that I saw Sir Robert die with my own eyes!*

Sir John leaned back in his father's chair. He looked nothing like the older man. He wore a neatly powdered white wig, a fine jacket patterned with flowers, and short velvet trousers. Steenie eyed the man with a mix of caution and suspicion. He never trusted anyone who was too heavily groomed.

Remembering his manners, Steenie bowed low to his front paws to offer the new lord of the castle his sympathies. "Greetings, sire. Steenie Steenson, here. I am sorry to hear of the death of yer father."

Sir John dabbed at his eyes with a lace handkerchief. Then he cleared his throat and sat up straight. "Yes, thank ye. Now, let us get down to business." He opened the thick, black rental book. He pointed to an entry. "Steenie Steenson, ye are listed here as owing a full year's rent."

"Oh, is that why I was called, sire?" Steenie wagged his tail eagerly. "It's a big mistake. I already paid it to yer father."

Sir John raised his eyebrows. "Ye have a receipt then, I'm sure."

"Uh . . . no," Steenie replied. "Actually, I had no time to get a receipt." *How should I say this? How about: Yer father was too busy making water boil with his feet and changing wine into blood? . . . Nope, I don't think that will work.* "As soon as I gave the bag of silver to Sir Robert, he became ill and passed on."

Sir John paused. "Well, that was unlucky, wasn't it? But maybe ye paid yer rent while someone else was in the room, then."

Steenie's tail slowed. *Wow! This guy doesn't give up. Well, I can play tug-o'-war just as well as anybody.* "Actually, Sir John, there was nobody else in the room except Dugal MacCallum, his servant. But as I just found out, he has followed his old master."

"Hmm . . . Yes. Another very unlucky coincidence," said Sir John. He stared at Steenie. "The man to whom ye paid the money is dead. And the man who saw ye make the payment is dead, too. Worse, the silver is nowhere to be found. How am I to believe what ye say?"

What does this guy want from me? Steenie's mind raced faster than a dog chasing its tail. Suddenly, he had an idea. "I know! Sire, I had to borrow from twenty people to come up with the rent money. They will be my proof!" He began to wag his tail in relief.

"I have little doubt that ye *borrowed* the money, Steenie," Sir John replied angrily. "It is the *payment* that I want proof of."

"But I *did* pay it! I did!" Steenie insisted. The fur on his neck bristled. He was insulted by Sir John's continued suggestions that he had not paid up.

"Indeed! Clearly ye wish to cheat me out of this money. If there is a word of truth in yer story, that money must be somewhere! Now, where is it?" Sir John demanded.

Steenie felt a growl beginning deep in his throat. "Where is it?" he repeated. "Where is it, ye ask? For all I know, yer father has it! Maybe he took it to the world beyond with him, along with his silver whistle!"

Oops! I guess I may have gone a little far with that last remark, Steenie realized. He looked up at Sir John, whose face was bright red with anger. *Uh-oh, angry lord of the castle looks as if he's ready to explode. This is probably a pretty good time to make my exit.*

Quickly, before Sir John could say a single word of response, Steenie turned and trotted out of the room. He dashed down the hallway to the staircase, skidding as he rounded a corner. *What is it about this place lately? Every time I come here, I end up running for my life. If this keeps up, I'll have to stop dropping by.*

Wishbone gathered his courage. *After all, I can't just leave the ball down there,* he decided. *The hero never gives up right in the middle of the rescue—even if it means staring straight into the face of evil itself!*

And that sure is an evil-looking face. Just look at the way it's scowling right at— Hey! Wait a minute!

The face in the center of the tree trunk had

changed. It was now grinning with a scary smile. Wishbone shook off a shiver. He took a deep breath. Belly in the grass, he began to move toward the tree.

This was the most frightening part of his mission, for sure. He would have to be brave. Just like Steenie Steenson . . .

Steenie raced out of the castle. He jumped on his horse and grabbed the reins in his teeth. He rode through the countryside at top speed. The Steenson family had lived on the Redgauntlet land for many years. Who knew what the rich landowner might do to Steenie after his angry outburst?

But how dare Sir John accuse me of not paying the rent! Steenie thought. *Now twenty of my best friends will want to be paid, and Sir John will, as well!*

Steenie was deep in thought. He forgot to pay attention to where he was going. Before long, he realized he had ridden deep into the forest. He was lost. He slowed his horse to a walk and looked around.

Steenie shivered. Night was falling, and he had no idea where he was.

Suddenly, Steenie's horse let out a frightened whinny. The animal reared up on its hind legs. Steenie clutched at the saddle horn with his paws, and he held the reins tightly in his teeth. It was all he could do to keep from being thrown to the ground.

"What is it that's spooking ye, laddie?" Steenie gave the horse a comforting pat on the neck.

Steenie's sensitive ears recognized the sound of

horse hooves in the distance. He saw no one for a while. Then, all of a sudden, a man on horseback appeared—almost out of thin air.

The man wore a dark cloak. His face was invisible in the shadow of the hood. Steenie sniffed the air, but the man had no scent at all.

"Helllooo?" Steenie peered at the hooded stranger. "Anybody home in there?"

But the man was silent as he rode up alongside Steenie.

"What is it ye want?" Steenie asked.

The man's voice was deep. "Tell me yer trouble. I may be able to help."

"If ye like, I will tell ye." So Steenie told the man his story. He left nothing out. He ended by describing his recent argument with Sir John.

When Steenie was finished, the man said, "Sir Robert is greatly upset by the harsh words ye said

about him to his son. But if ye dare to go see him, he will give ye the rent receipt."

"Go see *him?* Sir Robert?" Normally, Steenie would have laughed at such a remark. But something in the stranger's manner seemed serious—deadly serious. Steenie's fur stood on end. "Uh . . . it's not possible to visit the dead . . . is it? I mean, I've done my share of digging up old bones, but—"

"Follow me," the stranger commanded.

They rode on through the thickest part of the forest. After a while, the horses stopped in front of a large castle with dark gray stone towers and turrets.

Am I dreaming? Steenie wondered. *Redgauntlet Castle isn't anywhere near this part of the forest! And the castle in front of us is lit up and noisy with guests.*

At a high gate, the stranger waved Steenie on in the direction of the castle. He made no move to leave his own horse.

Steenie tied his horse to the gate. Then he walked up the familiar stone path to the castle door. As he walked, the grass growing between the stones crunched beneath his paws. He glanced down. *Hey! The grass is dry and brown!* He looked around. All the shrubbery surrounding the castle was dried up and brittle.

That's odd, Steenie thought. *I was just at the castle an hour or so ago. The grass was so green it was practically crying out for a good dig!*

He continued up the path and took the bell-pull in his teeth. This time the rope had a strange stale taste to it. As he pulled it, it crackled between his teeth. The bells rang inside the castle.

Almost immediately, the door opened. Sir

Robert's old butler stood in front of him! "Ah, Steenie!" MacCallum cried. "The master has been calling for ye!"

Steenie's eyes grew wide. "MacCallum! Are ye alive? I thought ye were dead!"

MacCallum lowered his voice to a whisper. "Watch out, Steenie. See that ye take nothing from anybody here. Not meat, not drink, not silver—just the receipt that is yer own."

Turn down food? Is he serious? Steenie shook his head and followed MacCallum into the castle. The great halls seemed familiar, yet somehow different. An unpleasant smell of mold and decay hung in the air. Steenie exhaled with a snort. He rubbed a paw against his nose.

Then he noticed something else. All the candles in the hallways were out. The candle holders on the walls held nothing more than stumps of wax with burned-out wicks.

But if there are no candles lit, why is it not pitch-dark in here? Steenie felt a shiver go down his spine. *Okay— major Creepy Castle Alert.*

MacCallum led Steenie to a great oak dining room. A group of more than twenty men was there at a big table, singing, drinking, eating, and yelling. By the side of the table sat Sir Robert.

No one paid any attention to Steenie. As he looked around, he recognized nasty faces from when he used to play the bagpipes at castle parties. He saw lords who had cheated their tenants; brutal men who had turned against their own families. *Whoa! Who made out this party guest list?* There were even men who, through their evil deeds, caused their own bloody deaths. Their wounds could still be seen.

139

Wait a minute! Steenie took another look at the frightening group. *These guys died long ago! They are all ghosts! Evil ghosts!*

Steenie froze. His four paws stuck to the cold floor. Then he heard a familiar voice thunder, "Steenie Piper! Come here!"

Steenie's paws felt like lead weights. But he forced himself to obey the command. Steenie approached the familiar voice with caution. He tried not to look at the faces of the dead men. Even so, he could see that their eyes glowed red and hot, as if sparked with fire.

Sir Robert was dressed in his dark velvet robe. He sat in his huge armchair, his feet propped up on the same cushioned stool. He looked the same as he had the last time Steenie had seen him on Earth—almost. The cushion for the monkey was beside him on the chair. But it was empty.

"What, hasn't the major arrived yet?" someone at the table asked.

"No, but he'll be here before morning," Sir Robert replied. He turned to Steenie. "Steenie, ye have come at last."

Steenie managed to gather the courage to speak. "Sir John will not believe I paid the year's rent unless I give him a receipt."

Chilling laughter burst out from the guests at the table. Their wild cries made the blood in Steenie's veins feel frozen.

And just what do they think is so funny? Steenie wondered. *A guy comes along and asks for a receipt, and suddenly they're all howling.*

"Ye shall have yer receipt," Sir Robert replied. "But play us a tune on the pipes first, Steenie."

Ye want me to entertain this group!? No, thanks! Steenie thought. "I-I don't have m-my pipes with me," he stammered.

"Well, then, ye may have something to eat and drink, Steenie," said Sir Robert.

Eat? Did he say "eat"? But then Steenie remembered the warning given to him by the old butler. He lifted his head bravely. "I came here not to eat or drink. I came to find out what happened to the money I paid ye . . . and to get my receipt."

Sir Robert let out a blood-curdling laugh.

The fur on the back of Steenie's neck stood on end. *There's that crazy laugh again. Okay, listen guys, the entertainment's just about over—ye got that?* He fought the urge to hightail it out of there.

"All right, then," Sir Robert agreed. He pulled a paper from his robe and wrote on it. "There is yer receipt, ye clever piper."

Steenie stepped forward and took the receipt.

"And, as for the money, tell my son to look for it in the Cat's Cradle," Sir Robert finished.

"The *Cat's* Cradle?" Steenie almost choked on the receipt in his mouth. He had no idea what that was, but he disliked anything involving cats. *Still, I suppose I'm lucky to have gotten my receipt.* He turned to go.

But Sir Robert roared at him again. "Stop! Here we do nothing for nothing. Ye must return here someday to pay me the respect ye owe me in return for the favor. I will expect ye to come back exactly one year from today. Remember, I am yer master."

But this was one command Steenie would not obey. He drew himself up on his four legs and looked Sir Robert straight in his terrible, glowing eyes. "Ye are *not* my master!" Steenie announced. "I am on the side of good!"

As soon as Steenie said the word *good,* he felt himself flying through the air. His paws flew over his head, and everything went dark. . . .

Wishbone gathered all the courage in his furred body. *Go, go, go, go—GO!*

He took a deep breath, then raced down the hill. He reached out and grabbed the ball in his teeth. As he did, he felt something brush against his back.

What's that? . . . Fingers! Fingers! Something's trying to grab me!

It caught hold of the Jack Russell terrier's collar. Wishbone shook himself from side to side, trying to loosen its grip.

Steenie stood up and shook the dew off his fur. *What happened?* he wondered. He'd awakened in Redgauntlet Castle's graveyard, next to the gravestone of Sir Robert. His horse was nearby. Then Steenie noticed a piece of paper on the ground beside him. The receipt! He grabbed it in his teeth and then ran to get on his horse. He urged the horse to ride through the thick mist in the direction of Redgauntlet Castle.

Steenie entered the castle and found an angry Sir John in the upstairs parlor. "Well, ye cheater," he said to Steenie, "have ye brought me my rent?"

"No, I have not," Steenie said, with the receipt in his teeth. He trotted forward and dropped the slip of paper on the table in front of Sir John. "But I have brought Sir Robert's receipt."

"What?" Sir John demanded. "But ye told me he had not given ye one!"

Steenie nodded toward the slip of paper. "Look at it carefully. Ye will see that it's right."

Sir John picked up the receipt and stared at it. His eyes widened when he saw the date. "What? The twenty-fifth of November! But that is today!" His eyes narrowed suspiciously. "Where did ye get this?"

"From yer father himself." Steenie told the whole story to Sir John. "And he said to tell ye that ye could find the silver in the Cat's Cradle."

"The Cat's Cradle? What does that mean?" Sir John demanded.

Steenie's tail drooped with disappointment. "Perhaps one of the servants might know?"

Sir John hesitated. "Steenie, if ye are lying, ye will be strongly punished."

The fur on Steenie's neck bristled. "On my honor, Sir John, every word I have told ye is the truth."

They questioned the servants and learned that "Cat's Cradle" was the name once used for an old turret of the castle. The turret, which towered above the castle, was now unused and in bad condition. It was reachable only by ladder from outside.

Sir John headed straight for the Cat's Cradle, and Steenie was right at his heels.

Steenie eyed the crumbling gray stone turret high above him. The ladder was old and rickety and missing a couple of rungs.

Sir John's eyes had a greedy, excited gleam in them.

Steenie stood in the damp grass as Sir John climbed the ladder to the top. Sir John opened the turret door. Suddenly, Steenie saw a dark figure burst out. He let out a yelp of surprise.

Sir John quickly leaned to the left, and the attacker flew through the air, yelling "Aaaaaaa-eeeeee-yaaaa!"

The dark shape came flying straight toward Steenie.

"Yikes! Large, dark screaming creature at twelve o'clock!" Steenie quickly stepped to the side.

The figure landed in the grass beside him.

"Hey, how about a little advance warning the next time yer thinking of dropping by?" Steenie said.

Suddenly, Steenie's nostrils were filled up with a familiar odor.

"Phew! I'd know ye anywhere, fella." It was the Major.

Standing over the monkey, Steenie was struck by a chilling thought. *Sir Robert's prediction came true. The Major will be joining him before morning!*

"I've found the silver!" Sir John cried from the turret.

Steenie felt a wave of relief go from his black nose to the tip of his tail. *But how did the silver get up there?* he wondered. *Was it the work of the Major? Or could it be some darker force?* Steenie shuddered, remembering the ghostly castle he had seen.

Sir John climbed down the ladder, the bag of silver in his hand. "Steenie, I apologize to ye for doubting yer word," Sir John said. "But I would rather keep quiet about this. I wouldn't want strange rumors to be spread about my family."

Strange rumors? Steenie thought. *Like what—that yer father is spending eternity in a ghost castle full of evil ghosts with burning red eyes?* But all he said was "Yes, sire." The truth was that he had no wish to speak of the terrible things he had witnessed.

"And as for this"—Sir John held up the receipt— "I think it is best that we put it quietly in the fire."

Sir John led Steenie back inside to the castle kitchen. He headed for the fireplace. Sir John held the receipt in his hand. Steenie watched as the man threw the paper into the crackling flames.

But to Steenie's great surprise, the paper would not burn. Instead, it flew up the chimney, hissing wildly. It left behind it a glowing trail of sparks. The sight of it sent a shiver up Steenie's spine. Suddenly, he remembered Sir Robert's command to return in exactly one year!

Steenie shook his head so hard his ears flapped. He was *never* going back to the castle of the evil dead— no matter what!

Wishbone, his soccer ball still in his mouth, managed to break free.

He turned and ran back up the hill as fast as he could.

When Wishbone reached the top, a cloud that had covered the full moon passed on. Suddenly, everything was brighter and clearer. Wishbone looked at the tree again.

Hey, there's no face, after all! That's just a twisted trunk!

The wind blew, and the tree's branches swayed, making a low moaning sound. One of the tree's lowest branches swept against the ground.

So that's what was grabbing me! This tree's not haunted, after all!

Wishbone turned and trotted away from the tree, the ball still in his mouth. He spotted a road up ahead. He knew just where he was now!

He took a moment to find a good place to bury his ball. He would come back for it when he didn't have a cat to chase. He carefully covered up the hole, then looked around for the sneaky black creature.

And there was that flash of the cat's black tail again!

Watch out, feline! I've got you now!

Wishbone was back in the chase.

Tails of Terror

6

"Passenger Pup on the Phantom Coach"

by Joanne Barkan

Inspired by "The Phantom Coach"
by Amelia B. Edwards

Illustrated by Lyle Miller

*N*ow that his soccer ball was safe, Wishbone could turn his attention to other, equally important matters—for example, that black cat. Finding the disappearing cat was testing his skills, but he was up to any challenge on that Halloween night.

Wishbone trotted along a narrow path in Jackson Park. It wound its way through the woods.

"Okay, cat, show yourself," the dog muttered. "I'm not here to play hide-and-seek. I came to chase you and catch you. I've got a mission, a cause, a higher purpose.

"Agh! I've also got an itch. A bad one. Got to scratch—*now!*"

Wishbone lay down on the path, raised his left hind leg, and scratched behind his left ear.

Ah! M-m-m, yes-s-s. What could be nicer than giving yourself a good scratch? . . . Oh, right. Someone else giving it to you.

As he scratched, Wishbone sniffed the woodsy air.

So, what's brewing around here? A fine blend of pine cones, dead branches, and moist earth. There's a hint of acorn, a dash of leaf rot, and—

The fur on Wishbone's neck suddenly stood up on end.

Cat!

The black form streaked past him. It raced off the path and headed into the bushes. Wishbone leaped up and ran after it.

"Bad sportsmanship!" he shouted. "Only a cat would take advantage of a dog who's sidelined with an itch!"

As Wishbone raced along, he noticed that a heavy fog was rolling in again. It gathered in the hollows. It seeped through the prickly bushes. It drifted into the bare treetops. Reflecting the moonlight, the haze looked thick and white.

Wishbone slowed down. *I can't see the cat. No wonder. This fog is almost like snow. It's hard to tell what anything is. In fact, it's impossible. In fact . . . I'm lost!*

Wishbone stopped walking. He turned slowly around in a circle.

Just stay calm. Think of a good, solid plan for getting out of here. Uh . . . like what? I know—find a familiar landmark. Such as . . . such as . . . Got it! That old stone wall must be around here somewhere. I'll find it and follow it. It'll lead me to the edge of the woods.

Wishbone walked quickly in what he hoped was a straight line. The fog swirled around him. He sniffed deeply, trying to catch the scent of damp stone.

Hmm . . . Lost outdoors at night. Fog as thick as snow. Searching for a stone wall. It all reminds me of— Oh, no! That really scary story called "The Phantom Coach"!

"The Phantom Coach" was written by the English writer Amelia B. Edwards. She lived from 1831 to

**1892. The famous English author Charles Dickens
first published her story in 1864 in his magazine,
called *All Year Round*.**

Staring into the fog in Jackson Park, Wishbone
imagined *he* was James Murray, a serious-minded
lawyer. He lived in London, England, in the last half of
the nineteenth century. He had a strange and terrible
tale to tell. . . .

My name is James Murray, and the story I am
about to tell is true. I've never told it to anyone before.
I dread telling it now. Well, let's be honest—just thinking
about it makes my fur stand on end.

The events took place twenty years ago, soon after
my twenty-fifth birthday. Yet, what happened then is
as real to me now as the four paws I stand on. You may
not believe my tale, but, please, don't try to convince
me it's not true. I've already made up my mind on the
subject.

Twenty years ago, I was in the far north of England
with my young wife. We had been traveling since our
marriage just four months earlier. Ah, how we loved
each other! How close and happy we were—like two
doves in a love nest, like two biscuits in a cozy basket,
like a pair of dumplings in warm broth . . .

It was early December, just days before the end of
grouse-hunting season. My favorite sport was search-

ing out those small birds that made their home in the harsh northern wilderness. I wanted to hunt. The feeling seemed to be in my blood.

My wife and I had arrived the previous evening at the simple inn of an isolated village. The village stood on the edge of a moor. Nothing is quite like that huge, empty, windswept land. Only prickly, low-lying shrubs like gorse and heather grow there. Only a lonely farmhouse, far from any other neighbor, shows any sign of human and animal activity.

An hour past dawn the next morning, I left the inn. My four paws carried me quickly onto the moor. I knew how hard the cold wind might blow. So I wore a loose, black-wool jacket over my vest, shirt, and fur. I pulled my round, felt derby hat snugly over the tops of my ears. I had wrapped leather gaiters around my back legs. They would protect my trousers from mud and water in the marshy places. I strapped my rifle and hunting bag onto my back. I hoped to carry a grouse or two home in that bag by late afternoon.

The hunt did not go well. Even with my sharp ears and super-sensitive nose, I caught nothing. Stubborn, I pushed on and on. The temperature dropped. The first snowflakes of a coming storm settled on my jacket. As the daylight faded, I realized my mistake. I had to face a most unpleasant truth: I was lost.

I shaded my eyes with one paw. I stared nervously into the growing darkness. The moor stretched on and on. In the distance, it seemed to rise up into low hills. Between the hills and me, I recognized nothing. Not a wisp of smoke from a chimney. Not a patch of farmland. Not even a sheep trail.

I soon realized I had only one choice: to walk on, hoping to find shelter. From muzzle to tail, I ached with tiredness. I forced myself to put one cold paw forward, then another. The tall, stiff bushes scratched my flanks. Worse than sore muscles, worse than scraped hide, my stomach was empty! I had eaten nothing since my morning breakfast of sausages and biscuits.

I walked on. The snow fell steadily, and heavily. The cold deepened. As the last bit of light faded, so did my chances of finding my way. My heart throbbed with pain when I thought of my sweet wife. At that very moment, my darling was waiting for me back at the inn. I could picture her standing at the window, so worried. When I had left that morning, she made me promise to return before dusk. How I wished I could keep my word!

I forced my legs to carry me forward through the

ever-deepening snow. Now and then, I stopped and shouted as loudly as I could. I prayed someone would hear my cries, find me, and lead me to shelter. The sound of my voice only made the silence afterward seem heavier.

A strange sense of fear came over me. I wasn't used to fear. It soaked into my fur like the wet snowflakes. I remembered stories of travelers hiking on and on in the snow. Tired and hungry, they would lie down to rest. "Only for a few minutes," they would tell themselves. Then they would sleep away their lives— and freeze to death.

How will I keep walking through this long, dark night? I asked myself. Will my four legs give out? Will my mental strength fail? Will I, too, sleep the sleep of death?

Death! A deep shudder rippled through the fur along my spine.

How terrible it would be to die now! I'm young—little more than a pup. Life lies so bright ahead of me! Work . . . friendship . . . food! And what about my beloved wife? Her heart will break—

I could not bear the thought. To chase it away, I howled louder and longer than ever before. When I stopped, my ears suddenly pricked up.

"What was that?" I whispered. "An echo?"

Once more I shouted. Once more I heard a faint response. A moment later, I saw a distant speck of light in the gloom. It flickered, then disappeared. It showed itself again—a little brighter.

I could wait no more. I ran toward the light. My four paws slid across the snowy ground. I halted only when my muzzle came within inches of a man's legs.

157

He carried a lantern. What joy! What relief! *Blech!* He smelled awful, but who cared?

"Thank heaven!" The words burst from my mouth.

The man lifted his lantern. "For what?" he grumbled. I could see that he was old. He squinted at me long and hard. He seemed to study every tuft of fur on my muzzle.

"Well . . . thank heaven for *you*," I answered. "I feared I would be lost forever in this storm."

"It's happened to others," the man said. "What's to stop you from ending your days here—if that's your fate?"

My fur bristled. "If that's *our* fate. If we're lost together, I must accept that. But, having found you, I will not be lost alone."

"You mean you'll follow me?" the man muttered.

I nodded so hard I almost lost my hat. "Yes. Correct. Exactly. Now, tally-ho! I assume you're on your way home."

"Maybe I am."

"Then I'm going with you," I said.

The old man's voice became angry. "And what right have you to force your way into my home?"

"It's my right to save myself," I said. "Suppose I were drowning in the sea. I would have a right to cling to your boat. Now I need shelter, water, and food. I can pay for your help."

The old man mumbled. Not even my sharp ears could make out what he said. He turned and began to plod through the snow. I leaped forward to catch up. Then I tramped along beside him.

After a few minutes of silence, my guide pulled a small, flat bottle out of his coat pocket. "Take a mouthful of this," he said. "It'll warm you up. You must need it since you're already worrying about freezing to death."

He uncorked the bottle and shoved it down toward my mouth. The sharp smell made my nose tingle and my eyes water.

"Whiskey!" I said. "No, thank you. On an empty stomach, I can drink nothing but water. Strong spirits like whiskey would send me into a tailspin."

My guide whistled softly. "We call whiskey and gin 'spirits.' But they're spirits that make the blood run warm. The *others* make the blood run cold."

He spoke in a low voice, as if he didn't want anyone else to hear him. This seemed strange, since we were completely alone.

I paused a moment, then asked, "What do you mean by 'the others'?"

He glanced down at me. The look on his face seemed to say *Hush, you fool!* Out loud, he said, "I mean spirits who walk the Earth. I mean spirits seen by men, women, and children since the world began."

He kept speaking in the same low whisper. That voice raised goose bumps on my hide. When the sound of his words had faded, I asked, "Are you talking about ghosts?"

"Indeed I am," my guide answered.

I suddenly felt relieved. I almost laughed as we walked on. "Ah, my dear fellow, I don't share your concern. I'm a lawyer. I deal with hard facts, not spirits. I deal with real causes and effects."

My guide grunted. "There are witnesses enough in such matters to make fools of a world of lawyers—"

I wanted to change the subject. I had other things

on my mind. "Pardon me. . . . Uh . . . may I ask your name?"

"Jacob."

"Well, Jacob, how far is it from here to the town of Dwolding? That's where I'm staying."

"A good twenty miles," Jacob answered.

Bitter disappointment made me sigh deeply. "Ah, woe is me. I can't possibly walk that far tonight—even if I rest for a while. My poor wife! She will worry herself sick until I return tomorrow. I would give anything to get back to Dwolding tonight!"

"Dwolding, eh?" Jacob said. "I suppose you could get back there tonight—*if* it's so important to you."

For the first time in hours, hope flooded into my heart. A shiver of excitement made my whiskers tremble.

"Nothing is more important to me!" I exclaimed. "Do you know a way?"

"I suppose I do," he answered. "The mail coach from farther north passes a crossroads about five miles from here. It's due to get to that spot in less than two hours. Then the coach goes straight to Dwolding to change horses."

My tongue hung out. I was panting with eagerness. "Take me to the crossroads, my good man," I said. "I will pay you well."

"I'll not walk five miles there and back in this weather," Jacob grumbled. "But I could take you to the old coach road. You could follow it to the crossroads. That's where the old coach road meets the new one."

I wagged my tail wildly. "Let's not waste another minute. Lead the way—I beg you!"

My guide grunted. Holding his lantern high, he

set off. I followed close upon his heels. We cast a single shadow on the snow-covered ground. Only the crunching sound beneath his heavy boots interrupted the silence. After fifteen minutes, the snow stopped falling. What lay on the ground by then reached more than halfway up my legs. My paws plowed through it.

Jacob wasn't exactly jolly company. It didn't matter, though. My thoughts raced ahead to the inn at Dwolding.

My darling wife, do not worry! I am on my way home to you. Soon, so soon, I will rest my weary head in your lap. I will wipe away your tears.

Such thoughts held my attention completely. I noticed nothing else. I paid no attention to the time. To my surprise, Jacob stopped after what seemed like only a few minutes.

"Just over there is your road," he said, pointing ahead. "A stone wall runs all along it. Keep the wall to your right side, and you can't get lost."

I pointed my muzzle in the same direction. "That's the old coach road?"

He nodded.

"And how far to the crossroads now?" I asked.

"About three miles."

I dipped my muzzle into my coat pocket. With my teeth, I pulled out my leather money purse. I gave Jacob a large gold coin. He became more friendly.

"Now, listen well," he said. "The old coach road is good enough for travelers on foot. But it was too steep and narrow for the mail coaches. Watch your step as you get near the crossroads. The stone wall is broken away there. It was never repaired after the accident."

"What accident?" I asked.

"Eh, one night the mail coach ran off the road," Jacob said. "It happened close to the signpost, near the crossroads. The coach flipped right over the wall. It fell a good fifty feet into the valley below."

"How horrible!" The back of my neck tingled. The fur there stood on end. "Were many lives lost?"

Jacob nodded. "Aye. All five men riding that coach, and the horses, too."

I gasped. "When did this happen?"

"Nine years ago," Jacob replied. "So watch for that signpost. It's a tall wood post. It's painted white. Just before it—that's where the wall is broken."

He pulled his flat little bottle of whiskey out of his pocket again.

"You'd best take a swallow of this," he said. "You've got three more long miles to walk."

With my mind still on the awful accident, I obeyed. I sat back on my haunches. I held the bottle tightly and tilted it to my mouth. The whiskey went down my throat like liquid fire. The old man's whiskey took my breath away.

"Aye-e-e!"

One swallow was enough. I gave the bottle back to Jacob. "H-h-hanks! H-h-ood h-h-ight!" I wheezed.

Jacob touched his hat—more or less. "Good night to you, too."

He turned and began to retrace his steps. I watched the light of his lantern. It slowly disappeared—swallowed up by the darkness of the moor.

I turned and started the next part of my trek. I soon found that I had no trouble walking along the old coach road. The sky above was a deadly shade of darkness. Yet the line of the stone wall showed up clearly against the snow. How silent it seemed. I had only the faint sound of my own paws padding on snow to listen to. How silent and empty! A strange, unpleasant feeling of loneliness crept over me.

Don't think about that terrible accident, I told myself. *Quick! Think of something pleasant. Recite poetry while you walk.*

> Humpty Dumpty sat on a wall,
> Humpty Dumpty had a great fall—

No, that won't do! Think of another one.

> Fe, fi, fo, fum!
> I smell the blood of an Englishman—

No, no! Try something else. . . . What else? Kings and queens of England—in proper order. Go on: Egbert, AEthelwulf, AEthelbald, AEthelbert, AEthelred, Alfred . . .

I had some success with this plan. When I reached King Henry V, however, the night air gave me a shock. It had turned even colder. I walked faster, but I found it impossible to get warm. My paws felt like ice. I lost all the feeling in my tail. My ears felt frostbitten under my derby. I was having trouble breathing. I felt as if I were struggling up the highest peak in the Alps.

Soon I had so much trouble breathing that I had to stop and rest. I sat upright, with my furred spine supported by the stone wall. I was panting painfully. From that position, I saw something that made my heart leap. Back down the road, I saw a distant point of light.

It must be Jacob's lantern, I thought. *He's come back to check on me.*

Even as I thought this, I saw a second light. It was next to the first. It came down the road at the same speed. I guessed what the lights were.

The lamps of a private coach!

Wishbone walked faster, still searching for the stone wall in Jackson Park. He concentrated on deep sniffing. At last, his nose tingled.

Okay, a new scent. Could it be . . . Yes, it is! Damp, old, moss-covered stones!

Wishbone leaped forward into the dense fog.

Here I go! Full speed ahead and— Ooof!

Wishbone ran right into something hard. He landed on his belly in a heap of dried leaves. His muzzle was pressed against a damp, moss-covered surface.

The stone wall! I knew I'd find it sooner or later.

Wishbone stood up. As he shook the bits of leaves and dirt off his fur, his ears pricked up. He heard a distant sound.

Cat again?

He turned his head in the direction of the sound. He saw a point of light. Then he saw a second one next to it. They looked fuzzy and faint in the fog. Slowly they grew larger. They were coming toward him.

Hey, what's going on here? This is just what happened to James Murray!

A private coach on the old coach road? I rubbed my eyes with my front paws. *Yes, those two lights must be coach lamps! But why would a private coach travel on such a dangerous road?*

I couldn't answer that question. I could only watch the lamps grow larger and brighter. The coach was coming up the road very fast. It moved silently through the deep snow.

A minute later, the body of the coach became quite visible. It looked strangely tall. A sudden hunch flashed into my brain.

Perhaps I've already passed the crossroads. Perhaps I didn't see the signpost. Perhaps I'm now on the new coach road. Perhaps this is the very mail coach I've come to meet!

I had no time to make any more guesses. The coach rounded the final bend. I could see the steaming breath of four gray horses, the driver, and the guard. The two lamps blazed like stars. They cast a haze of light around the entire coach.

I sprang forward. I stood on my hind legs. I waved my front paws in the air. Yes, it was the mail coach, and it approached at full speed. It passed me. I feared the driver hadn't seen me, but my worry lasted only a moment. The driver pulled the team of horses to a stop. I leaped toward the coach.

The guard was wrapped up to his eyes in capes and blankets. I guessed he was asleep, because he didn't jump down to help me. I hopped up and opened the coach door myself. I saw only three passengers inside.

There was plenty of room for me. I scrambled up the coach steps. I pulled the door shut behind me. I jumped onto the long seat that faced forward in the coach. I settled on my haunches in the nearest corner.

What good luck! I thought. *At last!*

Strangely enough, it seemed even colder inside the coach than outside. A nasty, damp smell made my nose twitch. *Phew!* I turned my attention to the other passengers. All three were men. All were silent. Each sat back in the deep shadows of his own corner. They seemed to be thinking, not sleeping. In need of company, I tried to start a conversation.

"How bitter the cold is tonight!"

I spoke to the passenger opposite me. He lifted his head, looked at me, but made no reply.

I tried once more. "I fear we are in for a harsh winter."

The lamps at the front of the coach cast little light inside. I couldn't make out the features of this passenger's face. Yet I could see that his eyes were still on me. His refusal to answer was rude. Usually this would have angered me. Suddenly, however, I felt too ill to react.

The icy-cold air had pierced through both my woolen coat and my fur coat. It had chilled me to the bone. The foul smell inside the coach was making me sick to my stomach. I shivered from muzzle to tail.

I turned to the passenger on my left. "Do you mind if I open a window? I need some fresh air."

The passenger neither spoke nor nodded. I lost patience and went into action. With one paw, I pulled on the leather strap that opened the window shade. The strap broke into pieces, as if it were made of stale, moldy bread. I noticed a thick coat of mildew on the window shade.

I turned my attention to the rest of the coach.

Good heavens! I thought. *It's in the last stage of decay!*

The wooden window frames splintered at the touch of my paw. A moldy crust covered the leather trim. All of it was rotting away from the woodwork. The floorboards were crumbling. The entire coach was foul with dampness and rot.

Like something the cat dragged in, I thought. *The mail-service people must have taken this coach out of an old storage barn.*

I turned to the third passenger, in the far corner. I hadn't spoken to him yet.

"This coach is in terrible condition," I said. "I suppose the regular coach is being repaired."

The passenger turned his head and looked straight at me. I shall never forget that gaze as long as I live. It made my blood run cold then. It makes my blood run cold now. His eyes glowed with a strange light. His white face was the face of a corpse. He pulled back his bloodless lips and showed me large, shining teeth.

A dreadful sense of horror rushed over me. My fur stood on end. I turned to the passenger directly opposite me. My eyes had gotten used to the darkness inside the coach. I could see that his face had the same whiteness. His eyes stared at me with the same strange light.

I rubbed my forehead with one paw and turned to the passenger next to me. Oh, heavens! How shall I describe what I saw? He was not a living man. . . . None of them was! An awful glow—the glow of final decay—

169

lit up their faces. Dampness from the grave soaked their hair. Their earth-stained clothes hung in shreds. They had the skeletal hands of corpses long buried. Only their eyes—their terrible eyes—were living. And all those eyes turned toward me with evil.

A-A-A-H-H-H!

I shrieked. A wild cry for help and mercy burst from my lips. I flung myself against the door. My front paws fumbled frantically to open it—in vain. In vain!

At that very moment, the moon shone through a break in the clouds. What I saw through the coach window made me howl with horror. I saw an entire scene as if in a flash of lighting. Time stretched out. I saw the signpost at the crossroads. It rose up like a terrible warning finger. I saw the broken stone wall . . . the plunging horses . . . the blackness of the valley below.

All the while, I heard a fierce screeching sound. It was my own voice!

The coach rocked like a ship tossed at sea. Next I heard a mighty crash. I felt a crushing pain. Then—darkness.

Wishbone watched the two lights approach through the fog. The sound that he had first heard became clearer. He recognized it.

Wheels! His heart pounded. He sucked in great gulps of cold air. *Is it a phantom coach? A phantom car? A giant phantom cat on roller skates? I'm not waiting to find out.*

Wishbone turned and began to run as fast as he could. He took long leaps. He bounded over puddles, over branches, over—*nothing!* He didn't see the ditch. Suddenly, he was tumbling through empty space. Down . . . down . . . *CRASH!*

When I, James Murray, opened my eyes, I felt as if years had gone by. Morning sunlight warmed the fur on my head. I saw my darling wife sitting by my bedside. She tenderly held one of my front paws. Tears of happiness streamed down her sweet cheeks.

I will skip over the emotional scene that followed. Briefly, I will report the story that my wife told me.

While walking, I fell through a break in a stone wall. This happened close to the crossroads where the old coach road met the new one. I landed in a deep snowdrift, which covered the rocks below. The snow had saved me from certain death. At dawn, two shepherds discovered me. They carried me to a shelter and contacted a doctor. When he arrived, I was ranting and raving, but not conscious. I had broken three legs and fractured my skull badly. My leather purse contained papers that revealed my identity and the name of the inn at Dwolding. The doctor got in touch with my wife. She came immediately to nurse me.

Thanks to my youth and sturdy body, I recovered. I never told my wife about the fur-raising events I lived through. I describe them here for the first time. Readers can decide for themselves what they *think* happened. I *know* the truth. Twenty years ago, I was a passenger on the Phantom Coach!

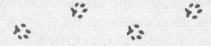

Wishbone heard voices, but they sounded fuzzy. He felt someone patting his head. Wishbone was on his back and he could feel the warmth of someone's lap. He was dizzy.

Where am I? Who's here with me? If I open my eyes, will I see the love of my life—the way James Murray did?

Wishbone slowly fluttered his eyes open.

Here goes. I see . . . Wanda? Wanda Gilmore! What's my next-door neighbor doing in Jackson Park at night?

Wishbone saw a second face. *Mr. Pruitt?* He was my buddy Joe's sixth-grade English teacher.

"Poor Wishbone," Wanda said. "You fell into that ditch and got the wind knocked out of you. But I think you'll be fine now. I'm just glad Bob Pruitt and I found you. We were bicycling home from the Oakdale Historical Society's Halloween bonfire."

Wishbone let Wanda put him into her bike's basket. She tucked a large scarf under him as a cushion. Then she and Mr. Pruitt started riding again. Wishbone could see that they were following the stone wall, which led out of Jackson Park. He snuggled against the soft scarf.

I'll be home before I know it. Could this really be the end of my Halloween adventure?

He sat up. "Wait a minute. I haven't caught that cat. What's more, I don't want this adventure to end. I *never* want an adventure to end!"

Wishbone got ready to spring—and he leaped out of the basket.

Tails of Terror

I

"No Noose Is Good News"

by Carla Jablonski

Inspired by "The Judge's House"
by Bram Stoker

Illustrated by Arvis Stewart

"Come out, come out, wherever you are!" Wishbone said in all directions. Wishbone was still winded from his fall in the ditch in Jackson Park. It was a good thing Wanda and Mr. Pruitt had found him. He was tired and tempted to go home, but he still had not caught that darned black cat!

Although the fog had lifted, clouds covered the moon and Wishbone could easily miss the cat in the shadows.

"What's the matter?" Wishbone called. "Oh, I should have known you were just an old scaredy-cat!"

"Mrrroowr!" With an angry howl, the black cat leaped out from under a bush. It raced out of the park.

"Hah! You won't get away from me this Halloween night! I'm the top dog!" Wishbone raced after the cat, leaving the park behind and running along the Oakdale streets.

Somehow the cat had already vanished. *Not fair. That cat had a head start,* Wishbone thought. "I may not be able to see you," he said, "but I can smell you!" He put his nose to the ground and sniffed. "Not my favorite aroma, either."

I smell car tires, autumn leaves . . . He wrinkled his nose. He wagged his tail. *Pizza straight to the right! Mm-mm!* He padded a few steps in the direction of the pizza smell, then stopped. *Nah! The trail's cold. That pizza was dropped on the ground at least four hours ago. All that will be left is a cheesy memory. Ha! Cheesy memory. Good one,* Wishbone told himself. *Now, where is that cat scent? . . . Ah—there it is!*

Wishbone trotted quickly, keeping his nose to the ground. He was determined not to lose the cat again. "Cat, cat, cat, cat," he repeated to himself as he followed the trail. He had to stay focused. There were so many interesting smells! "Cat, cat, cat— *OW!*"

What just hit me? he wondered, instantly on alert. *Oops!* Wishbone had been concentrating so hard he banged right into a fence.

Wishbone gazed up and saw a house behind the rickety fence. "Oh, no!" He gasped. "The Murphy house. Been here, done that." Wishbone had already had quite a fur-raising adventure in the abandoned old house. *It's easy to believe the rumors that this place is haunted,* he thought.

A movement at one of the broken windows caught his eye. The cat was slipping inside.

"There you are!" Wishbone dashed forward and raced up onto the rickety porch. He pushed the creaky door open with a paw and stepped carefully into the dark house.

"Oo-kay, this place still wins the creepiness award." He shivered under his fur. The light from the full moon shone in through the windows, creating strange shadows in all the corners. His ears pricked up.

The floorboards above him were creaking. *That must be the cat,* Wishbone told himself. He headed for the stairs.

Walking through the dark house set Wishbone's whiskers twitching. *Those shadows sure look . . . shadowy.* He shook his furred body hard. He tried to shake off the creepy feeling tingling from the spot on his tail to the tip of his nose.

There's nothing to be afraid of, he told himself. *There's nothing ever really hiding in the dark.*

He stopped suddenly and shook his head. *Yeah, sure! Tell that to poor Malcolm Malcomson! That's what he thought, until he learned otherwise.*

Wishbone glanced around the dark Murphy house. *In fact, this place reminds me of the scary house that Malcolm Malcomson rented in the terrifying tale "The Judge's House."*

"The Judge's House" is a story written by Bram Stoker in 1831. He's the guy who scared the world with his famous book *Dracula*. He did an awfully good job of scaring people with this story, too!

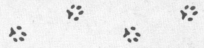

Wishbone sat back on his haunches on the old stairs. It was easy for him to imagine he was in the haunted house in that story from long ago. He pictured himself as a young math student, Malcolm Malcomson, in a little town in England. All Malcolm wanted was some peace and quiet so he could study for his big exams. He found a lot more than that.

Malcolm Malcomson wagged his tail as he gazed up at the old deserted house. It was a lonely looking place, surrounded by a high brick wall. Whoever had lived there must have valued privacy. It was nearly a mile from town. The best thing about it, in Malcolm's opinion, was that it wasn't in very good shape. It must have been empty for some time. That would mean he could rent the place cheaply.

"Perfect," he said. "Quiet, out of the way, and ugly enough to keep visitors away!"

Malcolm had arrived in the little English town of Benchurch the night before. To call it a "town" was a bit of an exaggeration. It had a single main street with a few shops, an inn, and a church. From the main street Malcolm could see rolling hills dotted with houses scattered in all directions. He set out first thing to rent a place to spend the summer. The quiet town and this house seemed ideal.

Satisfied with his discovery, he trotted back to the main street. Outside the rental-agency office, Malcolm checked his appearance in a window. He was wearing his second-best red waistcoat, along with his tweed trousers and yellow silk scarf. He wanted to make a good impression. He was nervous that no one would want to rent to someone so young. But it turned out he had no reason to worry. In no time at all, everything had been arranged.

"That rental agent seemed very eager to do business," Malcolm said. "The price was far below what I had expected." He headed back to the inn where he was staying to get his belongings. "Well, I suppose having an honor student stay in that old place will give the town some prestige. Why, if I get straight A's on my exams, maybe the townsfolk will put up a plaque— 'Math Genius Slept Here'!"

Malcolm's nails clicked on the wide floorboards of the inn as he crossed the front room. He leaped up on top of the desk and hit the little bell with his paw. Mrs. Witham, the owner, came out of the back room. Her big, hooped skirts swirled as she walked.

"Any luck, lad?" she asked. She was a cheerful, large woman.

Malcolm wagged his tail happily. "Yes! I found the perfect place. Would you be so kind as to help me settle into my new place? I've never been in charge of my own household. The place is huge, and I have no idea what I'll need to set up house." *I have a few ideas,* he thought. *Plenty of thick, juicy steaks. Maybe some meaty bones for study breaks.*

"Where is this marvelous mansion?" Mrs. Witham asked with a smile.

When Malcolm told her the location, Mrs. Witham threw her arms up. "Not the judge's house!" She gasped.

Malcolm's brown eyes widened in surprise. "Why not?"

The woman grew pale and grabbed onto the desk to steady herself. "That house has a history," she told Malcolm in a low voice. "More than one hundred years ago, it belonged to a judge. He was a terrible man. He handed down harsh and cruel sentences to those he tried. A 'hanging judge,' he was called."

"So that's why it's known as 'The Judge's House,'" Malcolm said. "But what's the problem now?"

Mrs. Witham shrugged. "I can't say for sure, but no one in these parts is willing to rent or buy it. Many people think the old place is cursed. Ooh, lad!" Mrs. Witham patted Malcolm's furred head in a motherly way. "If you were my boy, I wouldn't allow you to stay there one single night."

Malcolm thumped his tail on the desk. "Now, now," he assured the kindly woman, placing a comforting paw on her arm. "You have no reason to fear for me." He leaped down from the desk. "I am a math major. A student of logic. I don't believe in any supernatural or ghostly . . . feelings."

"I do hope you're right," Mrs. Witham said with a worried expression.

Malcolm left the inn to go hire a housekeeper. In a few hours he arrived at the judge's house. Mrs. Witham was waiting for him outside, holding a big basket of food. Malcolm smelled wonderful aromas.

"Why, Mrs. Witham," he called, trotting over to her. "I am surprised to see you here so soon."

"Well, I . . . I . . . that is . . ." she stammered, blushing slightly. "I wasn't very busy at the inn. I thought I'd help you set up your household."

Malcolm knew the woman was curious as a cat to see the inside of the judge's house. "You certainly brought plenty of food!" Malcolm said gratefully.

Just then he noticed that a sturdy older woman was approaching.

"Oh, here comes Mrs. Dempster. She has agreed to be my housekeeper."

Mrs. Witham glanced over at Mrs. Dempster. "She's not from around here, I imagine," she muttered. "Only a woman who hasn't heard the stories about the house would be brave enough to work in there."

Malcolm felt an odd tingle under his fur. A small feeling of fear. He shook it off. *Don't let local gossip scare you,* he scolded himself. Tail held high, Malcolm trotted to the partly opened front door of the house. He pushed the heavy door open with his paw and stepped inside.

"Ah-choo!" The moment he entered, Malcolm sneezed so hard his ears flapped.

"Agh!" Mrs. Witham shrieked outside. "It got him!"

"Nothing got me," Malcolm called out the front door. "It's just a lot of dust! There's absolutely nothing to be afraid of."

"Sounds like I've got some hard work ahead of me," said Mrs. Dempster, the housekeeper. Holding a feather duster and other cleaning items in front of her, she charged into the house. Mrs. Witham followed them inside.

While Mrs. Witham and Mrs. Dempster took care of setting up the kitchen and front room, Malcolm explored the enormous house. Every now and then he heard Mrs. Witham scream in terror and Mrs. Dempster cluck her disapproval.

What a shame such a once-magnificent house has fallen into such a bad state, Malcolm thought. By the time he returned to the front room, his white fur was gray with dust.

"We're all done," Mrs. Witham told him.

Malcolm glanced around the fairly clean room. A new bed was set up in the corner, and there was a pile of extra blankets on the dresser beside it. A single lantern was lit.

Malcolm held out his paw to Mrs. Witham. She was looking rather pale.

Mrs. Witham bent down and clutched his paw. He could feel her fingers trembling through his fur. She glanced around and shuddered. "Oh, lad, I don't like this place. Something is here, watching, waiting. I can feel it!" She shivered again and threw open the front door. "If you need anything, come to the inn," she said. Without a backward look, she turned and dashed out of the house.

Malcolm and Mrs. Dempster shook their heads as they watched Mrs. Witham hurry away.

"Silly woman." Mrs. Dempster gave a snort. "Those sounds—the creaking and the scratching? Rats and mice are what it is. Or loose floorboards and drafts blowing through cracked windows. Look around."

Malcolm did as the housekeeper said. He glanced all around the room.

"This place is more than a hundred years old," Mrs. Dempster said. "Of course it's going to have its noises. There's no mystery to that. Everything that happens has a logical explanation. Nothing to worry about here!"

Malcolm wagged his tail. He was glad that Mrs. Dempster had such a logical mind.

"Now, I'll just heat up your dinner. Then I'll be on my way," Mrs. Dempster told him.

"Excellent! I'll get right to work. I've lost a whole day of studying!"

Malcolm sat at a table and pawed open one of his textbooks. Right in the middle of figuring out what x to the third power might be, his nose twitched. His mouth began to water. He slammed the book shut. There was no way he could study with that wonderful scent floating in the room!

Soon Mrs. Dempster walked into the room and set down a tray. "I hope you'll enjoy your dinner. I'll be heading home now."

Malcolm immediately began to lap up all of the delicious beef stew. "See you tomowwow," he said with his mouth full.

Mrs. Dempster put on her coat and hat and left. Malcolm was now alone in the judge's house.

Mm-mm. Nothing like a nice hot, homemade meal to make a person feel cozy and safe, he thought. He licked the last drops of gravy from his whiskers. *Now it's back to studying for me.*

Malcolm sat in a high-backed chair at a table and read through his books for so long that the equations began to blur in front of his eyes. The room had grown dark around him, and the single lantern had burned low. *I may as well stop,* he thought. *At this point I wouldn't be able to tell the difference between a fraction and a fur coat.*

He let out a huge yawn. *I'll just rest my eyes.*

He shut his eyes and lay his muzzle on his paws. Now that he was no longer concentrating on his equations, he became aware of noises all around him. Lots of noises. Scratching, scampering, and squeaking noises above him, below him, beside him. He opened his eyes wide.

Hundreds of glowing eyes gazed back at him!

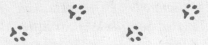

A pair of yellow eyes glowed at Wishbone from the top of the stairs in the Murphy house.

"Yikes!" Startled, Wishbone leaped up off his four paws and twirled in the dusty air. When he landed, he shook his furred body. "Snap out of it!" he told himself. *I was thinking so hard about the story of the judge's house that I forgot about the cat.* "Well, your little recess is over, kitty," he called. "I'm back on the case."

The eyes disappeared as Wishbone raced up the stairs.

"I know you're up here somewhere. You can't hide forever!"

A loud *meow!* came from below him.

Below?

Wait a second. The cat is downstairs? Wishbone poked his head through the wooden slats of the staircase railing. Then he pulled his head back in and scanned the upstairs hall. *If the cat is down there, then what was watching me from up here?* A shiver of fear ran through him.

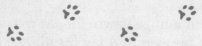

A shiver of fear ran through Malcolm. All those eyes! Staring at him. His heart double-thumped in his furred chest. He was too frightened to move. Then he remembered Mrs. Dempster's wise words: *Everything . . . has a logical explanation.*

Okay, think! Malcolm ordered himself. *Those eyes must belong to hundreds of . . . rats. Gee, knowing that makes me feel better. Sort of. Well, a little. More disgusted than scared. I think.*

With shaking paws, he leaned onto the table. He picked up the lantern's handle with his teeth and held it toward the wall.

His eyes widened in horror. Rats were everywhere! On the wooden trim around the ceiling and floor, on the furniture, on top of the picture frames, on the lamps—everywhere!

The rats froze for a moment in the light, then

scattered wildly. Within a few minutes they had all crawled back into holes in the walls. The room was empty again.

Malcolm lowered the lantern to the table. His heartbeat began to return to normal. *Well, they're more afraid of me than I am of them . . . as long as they don't come too close. Figuring out the value of x in all these equations is what has me worried! Not some silly rats.*

Still, I should let them know who's boss, he decided. *And it wouldn't hurt to have some more light in here. Not that I'm nervous or anything.*

Malcolm jumped down from his chair and lit all the lamps. He decided to light all the candles, too. He even built a fire in the room's big fireplace. Then, carrying the lantern in his teeth, he made his way around the entire room. He examined every nook and cranny.

Here and there he saw glittering eyes gazing back at him from a crack in the wall. As soon as Malcolm gazed back, the eyes would vanish with a squeak and a scamper. *Oh, yes,* he thought, his chest puffing out a little, *those rats know I'm in charge. They won't mess with a guy like me!*

He kept exploring the large front room of the house. "The paintings on these walls could use a good cleaning," he said. Dust covered the canvases so thickly he couldn't even tell what the pictures were of!

Malcolm held the lantern into a corner beside the fireplace.

"What is this?" A long, thick rope hung from the ceiling down to the floor. "This must be the rope that's attached to the bell on the roof."

With all the lamps, candles, and fire lit, Malcolm returned to his chair and table. He started to study his next set of math problems. He could still hear the rats scampering behind the walls.

Hours later, in the quiet hour just before dawn came, Malcolm finally closed his book. Something seemed . . . different. He realized the room was completely silent. Not a squeak out of the rats. Malcolm glanced up . . . and gasped!

Opposite him in a chair by the fire was the largest rat Malcolm had ever seen. It glared at him, as if Malcolm were its worst enemy. Malcolm shuddered. "Wow!" he said. "Talk about 'if looks could kill.'" *Gulp! Now, why did I say that?*

"Shoo!" Malcolm waved a paw at the creature.

The rat hissed, baring its fanglike teeth.

"If you're going to be that way about it! . . ."

Malcolm leaped down from the chair. He grabbed the fireplace poker in his teeth and charged after the rat. It scampered out of the way easily, climbing onto the mantel and out of reach.

Malcolm dropped the poker. *That rat doesn't scare easily!* he thought. *How can I get rid of it?* With panic rising in his furred chest, Malcolm threw math book after math book at the unmoving creature.

Malcolm lifted one final, heavy book in his teeth and flung it as hard as he could. The rat let out a horrified squeal. It climbed partway up the alarm-bell rope. Then it vanished through a hole in the middle of a large painting.

"And don't come back!" Malcolm shouted after it. "Now I know your hiding place. I'll be on the lookout."

He trotted over to pick up the book that had finally scared away the rat. He was startled to see it was the

Bible. *How very odd,* he thought. Then he put the unsettling thought out of his mind. After collecting all of the books, he was so tired he simply curled up in front of the fire and went to sleep.

The next morning Malcolm found it difficult to study. He hadn't even been able to eat a mouthful of breakfast—he knew he wasn't himself! He needed to get some fresh air.

When Mrs. Dempster arrived, he said, "I'm going to have lunch at Mrs. Witham's inn. While I'm gone, could you clean that painting?" He pointed a paw at the painting where the rat had disappeared.

If Mrs. Dempster was at all surprised by the odd request, she didn't show it in any way. "Certainly, sir," she told him.

Looking forward to Mrs. Witham's delicious cooking, Malcolm wagged his tail happily on the way to the inn.

"Oh, lad!" Mrs. Witham exclaimed as soon as Malcolm entered. "It's good to see you all in one piece! I mean to say . . . that is . . . well, I'm glad you're fine this day."

Malcolm waved a paw at her. "I'm fine, Mrs. Witham. You see, you were afraid for nothing."

"Afraid?" An older gentleman sitting at a table glanced up. "Did something frighten our dear Mrs. Witham?"

"This is the boy I told you about," Mrs. Witham said to the man. "He rented the judge's house. Malcolm, this is Dr. Thornhill."

"Ah, the judge's house." Dr. Thornhill studied Malcolm thoughtfully. He patted the seat beside him. "Please, join me."

Malcolm leaped up onto the chair. "Do you also believe that the house is somehow . . . wrong? Haunted, perhaps?"

"I have heard stories, certainly," Dr. Thornhill replied. "Have you had strange experiences there?"

Malcolm told the doctor about all the rats, and how difficult it had been to chase away the giant rat. "Finally, it raced up the alarm-bell rope and disappeared through a hole in a painting."

Dr. Thornhill raised an eyebrow. "The alarm-bell rope, you say?" He waited until Mrs. Witham went into the kitchen before he spoke again. "That rope is the very same rope the evil judge used to send poor souls to their death. He used it for each and every hanging!"

Malcolm felt his heart banging in his furred chest. "That's a very strange souvenir to put in one's house. Most people get a watch when they retire."

"Not this judge," Dr. Thornhill said. "Hanging people was his favorite part of the job."

Malcolm shuddered. "I'm glad I will never meet him."

Malcolm stayed at the inn far longer than he thought he would.

By the time he returned to the judge's house, the housekeeper had already gone. He grabbed a lantern handle in his teeth and hurried over to the large painting he had asked her to clean.

Malcolm stood in front of the painting with the hole in it. There in the dust-free frame was a picture of the very room he stood in. Malcolm recognized the fireplace, the high-backed chair, even the alarm-bell rope. And in the very center of the painting sat the judge. He wore a judge's red robe, trimmed in white fur. He was smiling cruelly.

I've seen those eyes before, Malcolm thought. *But that's impossible! The judge has been dead for more than a hundred years.* As the young math student studied the painting, he grew cold. He knew where he had seen those horrible eyes! They looked exactly like those of the giant rat!

Prickles of fear ran along Malcolm's fur. He whirled around. The large rat glared at him from the top of the high-backed chair.

Startled, Malcolm dropped the lantern. It crashed to the floor, sending the giant rat scurrying away. By the time Malcolm set the lantern upright, the tip of the rat's tail was beginning to disappear through the hole in the center of the judge's portrait.

That judge has nothing to do with the rat! Malcolm

scolded himself. *You're losing all sense of logic. The cure is to concentrate fully once more on your math books.*

Malcolm sat down for some long hours of hard work. He put all thoughts of rats and judges out of his mind . . . until the hour just before dawn.

Suddenly, he felt an urge to look up from the page. He did not know why. He scanned the room, then hopped down from the chair. *Of course. The rats are silent.* That's *what's different.* He glanced up at the portrait of the judge.

A feeling of cold terror swept through him. *This can't be,* he thought, his heart racing in panic.

The painting had changed! The entire center of the canvas had become blank. The figure of the judge had vanished!

Malcolm padded a few steps backward. His mind raced as he tried to understand what could have happened. *A painting doesn't just erase itself,* he thought.

He heard something behind him and whirled around. All four legs froze. Sitting in the high-backed chair was the judge himself!

Malcolm gasped. "This night has gone into creepy overdrive—from scary to terrifying, in nothing flat!" His ears flattened on his head. He had never felt more afraid in his entire life.

The judge just smiled a slow, evil smile.

"Did anyone ever tell you that there's a rat who looks just like you?" Malcolm said. "Oh. Right. It probably *is* you."

The judge leaned down and picked up the alarm-bell rope.

What is he planning to do? Tie me up? Malcolm watched the judge twist the rope in his fists.

"So, Judge," Malcolm said, slowly moving backward toward the front door. "I guess you want your house back. No *problemo*. I won't even bother to pack. Oh . . . and there's no need to return my deposit."

Malcolm's eyes widened when he realized what the judge was doing. The man was twisting the end of the alarm-bell rope into a hangman's noose! Malcolm glanced at the door. Just a few more feet.

"Well . . . don't worry," Malcolm said, his voice quavering with fear. "I won't be hanging around here anymore." *Oops! Bad choice of words.*

Malcolm whirled around and raced for the door. *Thwack!* The noose flew through the air and wrapped around the big bolt on the door. *Wham!* The judge yanked on the rope until the bolt turned and snapped shut.

Oh, no! I'm trapped!

The judge stood up.

Malcolm dashed behind a chair. His heart sped up as his mind spun. *He's going to lasso me and then hang me, just as he did to all his poor victims during his years as a judge. How can I escape? How can I stop his terrible scheme?*

Malcolm could imagine the rough rope wrapped around his neck. It would pull tighter and tighter, squeezing the life out of him. The image was so strong that Malcolm gasped for breath. He peeked his head out and saw the judge get up and remove the noose from the doorknob.

That is some long, long rope, Malcolm thought. He looked up to where the rope still hung from a hole in

the ceiling. He could hear faint ringing as the judge prowled around the room with the noose in his hands.

The alarm bell! Malcolm wagged his tail as he thought of one tiny possibility for escape. *If I could pull the rope, maybe it will bring help. It's a slim chance, but it's all I've got.*

The judge stood in the center of the room. He seemed to be in no hurry.

Ready, set . . . Malcolm wiggled the back end of his body, preparing to spring. *"Go!"* he yelled. He leaped forward and jumped up as high as he could. Startled, the judge stumbled backward. He tripped over a stack of math books. As he fell, he dropped the noose.

Malcolm quickly grabbed the rope and squeezed it in his teeth. He yanked it as hard as he could. He could hear the bell ringing loudly.

Behind him, he heard the judge getting to his feet, but he didn't risk glancing back. He planted all four paws hard on the floor. He put all his strength into pulling the alarm-bell rope.

"Malcolm!"

Malcolm's ears pricked up when he heard Dr. Thornhill calling his name from the front yard. Then came the loud noise of the front door being banged open. Dozens of footsteps clattered into the house. They burst into the front room.

"Malcolm! Malcolm!" Dr. Thornhill cried. "What happened?"

Malcolm finally released the rope. He looked around the room. The judge had vanished. Malcolm trotted over to the portrait. The image of the judge glared down at him. But he was no longer smiling.

Malcolm turned back to Dr. Thornhill. "I guess you could say I was saved by the bell!"

Malcolm gave the room one long, last look.

"Dr. Thornhill, will you help me pack my things?" he asked. "I'm going to spend the rest of the summer at the inn." He wagged his tail. "I don't feel like hanging around here anymore!"

Wishbone ran down the stairs. *I don't know who those eyes belong to, but I sure do know that cats say "meow." Instead of following my nose, I'm going to follow my ears.*

He heard a click-click-clicking sound coming from the next room. *This sure is a noisy house,* he thought.

He trotted into the dark room. *I can't see a thing! There goes that clicking again.* He whipped his head back and forth, trying to figure out what was making the noise.

Wishbone shot toward the sound. He grabbed a window-shade cord in his mouth. He tugged hard, then released it. *Thwap!* The room filled with moonlight as the window shade rolled up. The cat glared at him from across the room.

"Hello, kitty," Wishbone said. "Surprised to see me, aren't you?"

The cat squeezed through an opening in a broken door straight ahead. *Very clever,* Wishbone thought, coming to a stop. *I'll never fit through that hole.*

Wishbone wasn't going to let any cat outsmart

him. He pawed the bottom of the door. It opened a crack.

"Ha!" Wishbone barked in triumph. He shoved his paw, then his nose, into the opening. Finally, he pulled the door all the way open.

Wishbone stood in the doorway of a closet. The cat arched its back and hissed. Its ears lay flat on its head and its fur stood up straight.

"Looks like I've got you *just where I want you,*" *Wishbone said. He took a step closer.* There is no way this cat can get away from me now, Wishbone thought.

"Okay, kitty, it's just you and me." He was inches away, his alert body ready for action if his opponent made any sudden moves. His own fur bristled.

The cat let out a yowl. It pushed itself up against the wall. Its eyes never left Wishbone.

Wishbone studied the terrified creature. *It's not even a big cat,* he realized. He sat back and scratched the side of his head with his hind leg. "Aw, go on, get out

of here. Just don't tell anyone I let you go. I have a reputation to keep!" Wishbone stood to one side of the closet door.

The cat jumped up and raced out of the closet. Wishbone trotted to the front door. The cat had already vanished.

"Sometimes even a cat deserves a break," the dog said. "Besides, it is definitely time for some ginger snaps!"

Wishbone went outside, ran down the front steps of the old house, and headed home.

Tails of Terror

8

"Guard Dog of Haunted Hall"

by Vivian Sathre

Inspired by "The Open Door"
by Charlotte Riddell

Illustrated by Arvis Stewart

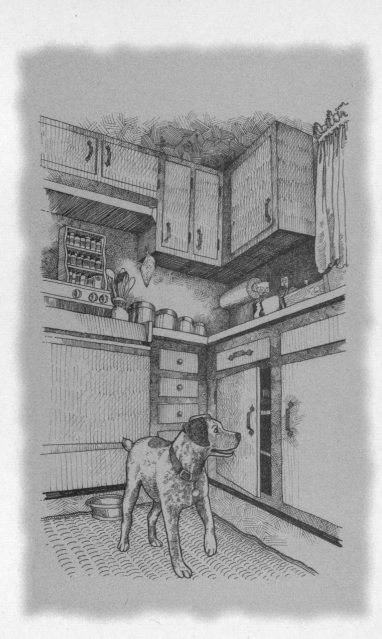

*W*ishbone pushed his way quietly in through the doggie door at the Talbot house. "Home at last. This is one tired dog." Chasing a black cat all night was challenging, especially with all the Halloween distractions. It was late. His best buddy, Joe, and Joe's mom, Ellen, were asleep upstairs. As Wishbone trotted into the dark kitchen, the only sound he heard was his nails clicking on the floor.

The faded scent of roast beef from dinner hung in the air.

"A bedtime snack would hit the spot. Maybe I'll just check my bowl one more time." Wishbone went over and looked into his bowl. "Empty. Okay, see you tomorrow for breakfast." As Wishbone turned to walk away, a muffled thump startled him. It came from inside one of the kitchen cabinets.

Wishbone pricked up his ears. Then, turning slowly, he looked around the kitchen. All of a sudden one of the cabinet doors began to creak open.

The fur on Wishbone's back bristled. "Identify yourself!" he growled into the dark.

The cabinet door stopped moving.

Wishbone's heart pounded. Wishbone leaned to

one side, trying to see inside the cabinet. But the door wasn't opened wide enough. "Helllooo! Show yourself. A hand, a foot—anything."

As Wishbone waited for a response, he thought about a ghost story written by Charlotte Riddell. The old story was powerful enough to send shivers down his spine. It was about a door in a mansion that would *not* stay shut. Staring at the slightly opened cabinet door in the Talbots' kitchen, Wishbone recalled the name of the story: "The Open Door."

Charlotte Riddell (Mrs. J. H. Riddell) wrote "The Open Door." She wrote a number of spine-tingling ghost stories, which were collected in 1882 and published in one volume as *Weird Stories*.

Wishbone, alone in the kitchen—or was he?—began to feel a little *weird* himself. He imagined *he* was Phil Edlyd, the young office clerk from "The Open Door." He worked for a company called Fryer's, a real-estate agent in London, England. The time was long ago—before electricity and cars were common—but *ghosts* had been around for a long time.

"Phil!"

I looked up over my typewriter. A fellow clerk

much older than I was hurrying my way. I straightened my crisp white shirt and houndstooth vest.

"I know how you can lay your hands on some extra money. Two pounds."

My ears pricked up. Why, for a whole year's worth of work at Fryer's, I received only twenty pounds! It was very low pay. I was always in need of money. My mother and sisters were forever putting on the dog—living far beyond what we could afford. Bill collectors were always snapping at our heels.

"Go on," I said, wagging my tail with curiosity.

The other clerk moved the unlit candle on my desk out of the way. Then he leaned down on my desk and looked me right in the eye. "You know that big house we rented to Carrison, the wealthy business-man? Well, the fellow signed a long lease, but he says he's unable to live there." The old clerk raised his eyebrows and nodded toward the boss's office. "Fryer said he would give two pounds to anyone who would go to the house and find out the reason why Carrison won't live there."

I put one of my front paws on my desk and wagged my tail. "Where is this place?"

"You mean Ladlow Hall? I know very little about the property. Fryer said Lord Ladlow—the owner—was out of the country. The house is just a train ride away—in the heart of the animal-grazing countryside."

Grazing country! My tail thumped against my chair. How wonderful. I imagined running free on a grassy hillside instead of weaving my way through the crowded city streets of London. And I would be getting paid for it. The whole idea sounded too good to be true. "And what *is* the matter with the place?" I asked suspiciously.

A strange look appeared on the other clerk's face. "There's a door in one of the rooms that won't stay closed."

I stared at him. "You're kidding, right?"

He shook his head. "Not at all. Carrison came into the office earlier to get out of his lease. Fryer went into a terrible rage and refused to do it." The clerk straightened up and waved a hand toward the front door. "That's when Carrison stormed out to talk to his lawyer. If Carrison has to, he will force Fryer into court to get out of his lease."

"So tell me—" I took a moment to scratch under my stiff collar with my hind paw. "Why won't the door stay shut?"

The old clerk's eyes darkened. "People say that it's because the mansion is haunted."

"Helllooo!" I eyed him. "There are no such things as ghosts!"

"Then you are just the right person to do this job," he said. He took his pocket watch out of his vest and looked at it. Then he quickly slipped it back in place. "I have an appointment across town. I'll be late if I don't leave right now." He smoothed the sleeves of his suit jacket, took his hat down from the hat rack, and left the office.

Looking out the window, I watched him disappear into the famous milky-white London fog. I thought about the two pounds. With them I could easily afford to buy a few extra treats. First I'd purchase a new umbrella for my poor father. Then I'd go to the butcher shop and pick out a nice big meaty bone for myself.

I remembered how much rent Mr. Carrison agreed to pay for Ladlow Hall. It was a big sum of money. Surely Mr. Fryer would give more than two pounds to get the ghost out of there and keep Mr. Carrison happily paying rent. Maybe Mr. Fryer would give me ten pounds! Or twenty!

Gathering courage, I jumped down from my chair and trotted into Mr. Fryer's office. The flame rising from the lamp on his desk gave a warm glow to the room.

"What is it?" He looked up from his work just long enough to dip his pen in the inkwell.

"Sir, I'd like to have a chance to solve the mystery at Ladlow Hall," I said boldly. "I'm not afraid of big, empty houses, and I do not believe in ghosts. As for burglars . . ." I wagged my tail. "Well, chasing them away is in my blood!" I barked proudly. "But I should like more money to do the job, sir. Perhaps you could offer a ten-pound note?"

Mr. Fryer looked me squarely in the eye. His face reddened. "How dare you—a lowly clerk tell me *I* should give *you* more money?" He stood and opened the company's cash box. "Here are the last of your wages. You're fired. Now get out."

"But—"

"Go!" he ordered me, pointing to the front door.

My heart was in my paws. Not only would I not get the two pounds for going to Ladlow Hall, but I no longer had a job. That meant it would be the responsibility of my father to pay *all* the bill collectors himself.

And Patty, my sweetheart—what were her parents going to think of me now?

I stood on my hind legs, took my hat from my desk, then walked outside slowly. I shivered from my muzzle to my tail. The fog was like a cold, wet blanket draped around my shoulders. I wandered the busy streets for more than an hour. Then, all at once, an idea came to me. I would try to make a deal with Carrison, the fellow who had rented Ladlow Hall.

I trotted down the street and went into Mr. Carrison's office. Then I made my offer to him. I sensed the man took a liking to me right away. But still he asked for the name of someone who could guarantee my honesty and speak for my good character.

"Robert Dorland, my uncle," I said.

He looked surprised. "Robert Dorland?"

I nodded.

"Why, my company has done business with the

man! Come." He grabbed his hat and coat. Before I knew it, he led me down the cobblestone pavement and into my uncle's office. Quickly he told my uncle why we were there.

"He is trustworthy," my uncle said of me, getting out of his chair. He walked to a fireplace and turned his back to the empty grate. The look on his face was serious. He was pale. His eyes locked on mine. "Have nothing to do with this, Phil. Don't get involved with this ghost-hunting and spirit-finding."

"But I'm not afraid," I said.

"You don't believe in ghosts, do you, Mr. Dorland?" asked Mr. Carrison with a slight sneer.

"Don't you?" asked my uncle.

There was a pause. Mr. Carrison fidgeted. "If you ask me the question here, in the heart of the lively city, my answer is *no*. Yet the strange door at Ladlow Hall is beyond my understanding. I can't live in Ladlow Hall, and I can't convince anyone else to live there, either."

Mr. Carrison offered his hand to me.

"Ten pounds—do we have a deal?" he asked me.

"Yes!" I gave him my paw to shake.

We went back to Mr. Carrison's office. There he gave me expense money and the key to Ladlow Hall. "You have two weeks to get the door to stay shut. And you must write me every day to keep me up to date." He stared at me for a moment. "If at any time you feel the job is too much for you, give it up."

I wagged my tail. Mr. Carrison gave me a hearty pat on the back. Then I left.

Early the next morning I was on my way to Ladlow Hall. A borrowed revolver was in my jacket pocket. My rifle, along with a pack of personal items, was strapped to my back. My worried uncle, my sweet Patty, and Mr. Carrison, who'd rented Ladlow Hall, were the only three people who knew where I was headed. I told my family only that I was going out of the city on business. Not one word about ghosts had escaped my muzzle.

I rode the train as far as the last stop. Then I started out on my paws. It was a sunny but cold walk. Yet the fresh country air gave me energy. I raced through the fallen leaves that covered the narrow lanes, barking for joy. Sometimes I stopped to sniff a tree or roll in the thick green grazing grass. I never wanted to go back to London. The countryside was where I was meant to be!

I walked on, but I was not sure which road led to Ladlow Hall. Finally, I asked for directions from a gentleman riding a large horse. But I made sure to stay away from the horse's hind feet so I wouldn't get kicked.

With his riding stick, the man pointed over a thin iron fence. "That road over there leads to Ladlow Hall."

"Thank you," I said, staring at the gentleman's thick fur coat collar as he rode off. I sensed the man was important in some way.

I trotted to the road and saw that it was uphill travel all the way. At least the route was lined with trees! My walk was long, but finally I stood, panting, in front of Ladlow Hall. It was a large, old-fashioned country house, three stories high. The trees that surrounded the house kept it in dark shadows, even though the day was sunny.

I cocked my head and listened, but I heard nothing,

even with my superb hearing. How strange! Silence hung over the place like a cloud. Well, I would change all that.

"Helllooo!" I trotted up the porch steps. I noticed the shades were pulled down in the front windows. Taking the key from my pocket, I unlocked the heavy front door. "Yoo-hoo!"

I went into the foyer—the huge entry hall. It was so big that there were two fireplaces there for burning wood. I'm sure both were needed; the black-and-white-marble floor was as cold as ice against my tired paws. Facing me, a grand curving stairway led to the two upper floors. I set the revolver on a side table. Then I glanced around the hall, amazed. The walls were decorated with old pictures, animal horns, and antlers. Statues filled nooks in the walls. Suits of armor stood in the corners like guard dogs.

"And look at all the doors!" Never in my life had I seen so many doors together, leading to so many different rooms! Two of the doors stood open—one wide, the other just a bit. I put my nose to the floor and cautiously sniffed my way closer. Suddenly, the fur on my back stood on end. Mr. Carrison had never told me *which* door refused to stay closed, but I sensed it was one of these two.

Quickly, I closed one door, then the other. Both were made of heavy oak, and they had good locks and solid handles. I was satisfied the doors were closed tightly.

With my pack still strapped to my back, I trotted up the staircase to the second story. "Helllooo! Anybody home?" My steps echoed. I felt like an intruder. Walking up and down the hallways, I found only a few of the bedroom doors open. But I sniffed out every one. Most were completely empty. Some had a few old chairs and dressing tables, but no personal items such as clothes or books. Shutting each door tightly behind me, I locked those that had keys.

"Going up!" The stairs creaked as I climbed them to the third floor.

There were no attic windows overlooking the front yard of the house. I put my front paws on a sill of a side window and looked out. I saw that the sun was starting to go down. Oh! Below was a garden! I wagged my tail. Digging in that dirt was going to be a real treat!

I trotted over and checked out a window overlooking the back of the house. Pay dirt! The land was thick with trees! What more could a guy ask for? Then, as the sun sank even lower, I realized what a huge old house this was for one person. As I turned to go downstairs, a shiver went down my furred spine.

I hurried down to the ground floor. I wanted to explore the whole house before it got dark out. That was the bad thing about trying to do my work late at this time of year—it got dark so early. I dashed through some sitting rooms, the servants' wing, the pantry, and the coal cellar, shutting doors behind me as I went. Nothing seemed odd or out of place. The doors in the kitchen, too, were shut tight.

My next stop would be the living rooms. As I trotted into the darkening front hall, I felt *weird*. Those hollow, ghostly suits of armor gave me the creeps. The statues did, too. Without the sunlight, they looked icy and unfriendly—almost threatening. I threw a quick glance over my tail, then trotted faster through the mansion.

"Maybe I'll just save the rest of the first-floor rooms for tomorrow. I'll choose a room for sleeping, make a fire, then lie down and get some solid rest." I wagged my tail. I was starting to relax just thinking about taking a load off my paws!

Then, in the dim light that remained in the front hall, I glimpsed the two doors I'd shut when I had first arrived. I froze in my tracks. A low growl escaped my throat. One of the doors stood wide open! I blinked, then looked again. Nothing had changed. But that was impossible—I'd shut the door myself!

I told myself not to be afraid. My sharp instincts quickly kicked in. This is what I had come here for—to uncover a puzzling mystery.

"Okay, one more time." I shut the door. "Now, I'm just going to walk down the hall . . ." Looking straight ahead, I walked to the grand staircase. Then, turning, I walked back and looked at the door.

It stood wide open. . . .

A faint scratching noise—so low that Wishbone barely heard it—came from the kitchen cabinet. Wishbone stepped back. "Come out and face me like a . . . like a . . . mouse, or ghost, or—whatever you are!"

Wishbone eyed the cabinet, but nothing happened. *Okay, it is time for a reality check for the cute spotted dog!* He slowly wagged his tail and looked around. *I can't see anybody else right now because I am the only one in the kitchen.* Wishbone turned to walk away. Something bothered him. *Unless whatever opened the cabinet door is a ghost. Then it could open the door without my being able to see it at all!* Wishbone stopped wagging his tail.

Maybe what's happening to me is a repeat of what happened to Phil, in "The Open Door"!

Staring, I knew for sure that *this* was the room with the open door.

Ignoring the shiver running down my spine, I entered the room cautiously. I went directly to the windows—there were two of them—to pull up the shades. But they were set high, out of my reach, even when I stood on my back paws.

Little moonlight got through, so I lit a candle. I saw that a rug covered part of the darkly polished oak floor. A bookshelf stood on one side of a fireplace, and a cabinet was on the other. An old chair, its cloth covering now faded, sat nearby. It was a dreary, gloomy room with dark, paneled walls. Ugly velvet drapes hung from near the ceiling to the floor.

On the wall directly opposite the opened door, there was a bed. The purple-silk covering on the bed looked just like a cloth that would be laid over a coffin. I shuddered. Next to the bed was another door. I tried to open it, but it was locked. I couldn't help wondering why—none of the doors inside any of the other rooms had been locked.

Stepping out of the room, I shut the door. There wasn't a key to lock it, so I just walked away. Three steps later I spun around. The door was open.

As I stood looking toward the room, fear nipped at my paws. "Helllooo!" I said to myself. "Get a grip. This is the mystery you have come to solve!"

Standing tall, I glared at the door.

"Stay open, then!" I barked. "I've had enough of you for one day!"

I chose a room farther down the hall to use as my bedroom. I took off my backpack. I quickly wrote two letters—one to Mr. Carrison, the man who had hired me; and one to my sweet Patty.

Then I left the house and walked down the long path that led to the main road. It wasn't yet supper time, but it was as dark as midnight. The wind had started to howl, and the cold air bit at my ears and muzzle. Moonbeams coming through the tree branches cast monstrous shadows on the ground around me. The shadows jumped and gobbled up one another as the wind blew the branches back and forth. I let out a bark, snapped at the biggest shadow, then trotted on.

The nearest post office was in the village of Ladlow Hollow. The postmistress was standing by the front door. I wagged my tail. "Hello," I said politely.

"Hello," she replied. Then her eyes looked over my head and she smiled.

I turned my head and looked back over my tail. Walking past me on foot was the gentleman who had given me directions earlier—the important-looking man on the horse.

"Good evening," he said to me. Then he nodded to the postmistress.

She curtsied. I wished him a good night.

Her eyes followed him in the dark. "His lordship is looking very tired," she said.

"His lordship?" I was puzzled.

She nodded after the fellow. "Aye. Lord Ladlow."

Lord Ladlow! I thought he was thousands of miles away.

As I made my way back to the mansion, I thought about Lord Ladlow being right there in the village. *So, why,* I wondered, *am I the one staying in his spooky house?*

When I got halfway up the path to the old place, a nearby bush rustled. A split-second later I ran through the underbrush, chasing whatever had been hiding there. Unfamiliar with the land, I stumbled over a branch in the dark. Whatever I was chasing shot out and raced into an area thick with bushes.

I followed. As I crunched through the branches, I tried to avoid falling into dips and holes in the ground. I didn't want to twist a paw and get stuck outside all night in the pitch-blackness. Panting, I finally stopped and sniffed the air. But any scent I was hoping for was carried off in the wind. I barked out in frustration, then made my way back to the house.

The armor and the statues in the huge hallway looked unfriendly as I entered the mansion. And *the door* was still open, but I was tired. I decided not to investigate it further that night. I picked up my rifle from the hall table. It was wet! And it had been unloaded! Glancing around, I saw moisture on the floor, too. I couldn't help myself; I flipped in the air. I was excited. I was dealing with something very real—made of flesh and blood!

I trotted to my room, locked my door, and went to sleep.

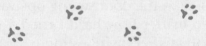

The next morning I was up with the birds. *The door* was open, just as I had last seen it the night before. I ate some of the food I'd brought with me—mostly meaty bones, a great snack, and full of vitamins. As I sat in the entry hall, thinking about my situation, the mail carrier came by with some letters. I opened the door and greeted him. He was wet from the drizzle, and he was shivering.

"Thank you!" I wagged my tail as he handed me the mail. "I'm sorry if coming all the way out to the Hall is a problem for you."

"No, sir, it's not," he said, his breath making white puffs in the air. "I pass by here every morning on my way to her ladyship's."

I cocked my head. "Who is 'her ladyship'?"

"Lady Ladlow," he answered. "The old lord's

221

widow. She lives about a quarter of a mile from here—through the shrubbery and across the stream."

"I see. . . ." I nodded that I understood, and the man left.

I tore into a letter from Patty, devouring every word as if each was the best cut of meat. I wagged my tail faster than I had in a week! Then I opened a letter from my uncle. He begged me to come to my senses and leave Ladlow Hall before anything bad happened. I sighed, then put his letter out of my mind.

For the rest of the morning, I gazed at the door from inside the room and out. I learned that if I stood near the door, it stayed closed. But if I took three steps across the hallway, the door swung open wide. *Why?* I wondered. No matter how hard I tried, I couldn't dig up any clues to answer my question.

At two o'clock my investigation was interrupted by a visitor. I opened the front door. There stood Lord Ladlow! "Please, come in," I said.

He shook his head. "Walk with me across the grounds," he said kindly. "I want to talk to you."

Puzzled, I cocked my head, then joined him.

"You must be told about all of the rumors that are going around." He clasped his hands behind his back as we walked. "Of course, when I had Fryer, the real-estate agent, rent the place to Carrison, I knew nothing of the open door."

"You didn't, sir? Uh . . . I mean *my lord.*"

He waved his hand to stop me. "No need to use my title. Speak to me like a friend." He went on. "I had no idea there was a ghost story connected to Ladlow Hall. Is the story the reason you're here?"

As I explained my situation to him, he nodded with interest.

"What have you seen so far?" he asked.

"A door that won't stay shut, and there's no earthly explanation for it." I sat down to scratch my side.

"Are you frightened?" There was concern in his voice.

"Not since I found that my rifle had been emptied. It seems someone is afraid of a bullet." I looked up at him. "I don't think a ghost would be afraid of being shot."

Lord Ladlow waited until I stood, then began walking again. "I feel I should warn you. The people of Ladlow Hollow have a theory about the open door."

This I had to hear! "And what would that be?"

"Since that was the room my uncle was brutally murdered in—"

"Murdered!" A chill raced down my spine.

He nodded and kept walking. "Two years ago, my uncle was murdered sitting in his chair in that very room—the room with the open door. The murderer has never been caught. At first, many of the people around here thought I was the one who had killed him." He looked off into the distance. "Indeed, some still think I'm the guilty one."

"Uh . . ." I wagged my tail nervously. I sensed Lord Ladlow was as loyal to his family as a dog. But what if I was wrong? I could be in real danger here! "You didn't kill him . . . did you?"

"No, lad. I loved the old man. I felt close to him even after he married a young woman and took me out

223

of his will—except for leaving me Ladlow Hall." Lord Ladlow pulled his fur collar up around his neck to keep warm. "Then one night my uncle sent for me. He told me he was making things right again, putting me back in his will. Everything he owned was being left to me."

Lord Ladlow slipped his hands, all red from the biting cold, into his coat pockets.

"My uncle said we'd talk more about the changes in the will the next morning. Then he wished me a good night."

I watched a squirrel run up a nearby tree as I waited for the lord to tell me more.

Taking a deep breath, he spoke again. "In the middle of the night, everyone in the house was awakened by a scream. It was horrible. We found my uncle, dead in his chair. He'd been stabbed in the back of the neck while writing a letter to me."

I cocked my head. I still seemed to be missing some very important information. "What was in the letter?"

"My uncle wrote that he wanted to tell me his

reasons for changing his will. He wrote that it had something to do with his honor. The last line he wrote read: 'In the letter you will find sealed up with my will in——.'" Lord Ladlow stopped, turned, and started back across the wide lawn. "Then he was stabbed. Some thought that I did it out of revenge for being cut out of the will."

"But he'd just put you back in," I said, puzzled.

"Yes," said Lord Ladlow. "But no one else knew it at the time. Then the next day my uncle's lawyers told everyone that three days before his death, my uncle *had* willed everything to me."

My paws were getting numb from the cold; I walked faster. "And some people still think you killed him?"

"My uncle was very rich." He looked down at me. "My lady—that's my uncle's widow—pointed out that if my uncle did leave everything to me, I had an even better reason to kill him. She and her lawyers have been trying to prove that ever since his death." Lord Ladlow pulled his hands out of his pockets and breathed his warm breath on them. Then he slid them back into the shelter of his coat. "I hired my own lawyers to fight back. But until the matter is settled, I can't touch any of my uncle's money."

It was clear to me now. The lord was in a no-win situation. At first, people had thought he killed his uncle for revenge; then they thought he did it for money.

"When I lost my good name, I lost my good health. I left England and turned Ladlow Hall over to the real-estate agent, to rent out. He rented the place to Carrison. When I returned recently, the agent said

225

Carrison was refusing to pay the rent." Lord Ladlow pointed off to a pond, and we headed in that direction. "Now that I've learned of the open door, I'm sure that's why. I'll let the man out of his lease immediately."

My heart sank to my paws. "Does that mean my services are no longer needed?" *Had I lost my job and the ten pounds?*

We stopped to watch some ducks swim. Any other time I would have given them a run for their money!

Lord Ladlow's eyes darkened. "It's very important to me that this ghostly mystery get solved. If you are not afraid, stay on. I'm too poor to promise you anything, but I would be very grateful for your help."

My tail sliced back and forth through the air. "Oh, my lord! I don't want any more money. I want to show Patty's father I'm good for something—"

"Who's Patty?" he asked.

"My sweetheart."

Lord Ladlow smiled as if he understood. After a brief silence, he spoke again. "I'll be away for a few days. When I return, I'll come by and check up on you."

I nodded. As we walked on, I mentioned that someone had been hiding in the bushes the night before.

"It could be hunters," he said. "But don't take any chances. Someone might want to harm you—or worse. Maybe poison you." His face once again took on a serious look. "Don't trust anyone. I suggest you keep your food locked up, and drink only water that you have pumped yourself from the well."

I agreed. We parted, and I trotted back to the house.

The first thing that I did when I got inside was

shut *the door*. Then, wanting to build a fire, I started toward one of the fireplaces in the front hall. Suddenly, I spun around. *The door* stood wide open once again.

I spent the whole day giving that door my full attention. I didn't even go out and dig in the gardens. And if I shut the door once, I shut it a hundred times. As long as I stood nearby and looked at it, the door stayed shut. But as soon as I turned my back and took three steps away, it mysteriously opened! This couldn't even be blamed on some stray cat!

That evening, I locked my food away in the pantry. Then I walked back and forth, time and again, in front of the open door. *Think, man, think. How can you get to the bottom of this mystery?* I shivered every time I thought about the murder.

Finally, when I was almost too tired to think, I got a strange idea. I went to the stable behind the house, where my horse would be kept—*if* I had a horse. I searched underneath the whips and harnesses hanging on the wall. I found some sort of tool that looked like a heavy spike. After grabbing a hammer, I carried them both back into the house.

I went directly to the open door. "Now *I* am keeping you open!" I barked. With all my strength, I pounded that spike into the floor.

After going to my room, I curled up in the middle of my bed. I fell asleep wondering why I'd just spiked *the door* open.

In the morning when I awoke, I trotted down the hall. *The door* was shut tight! The top part of the spike I'd hammered on the night before lay on the floor in the hallway. I opened *the door*. The fur on my back

stood on end. The point of the spike, which I had driven deep into the floor, was still wedged in place.

What in the world is going on in this place? I wondered. Suddenly, my collar seemed too tight; it was hard to breathe. I hurried outside to the porch, held my head high, and breathed deeply. Soon the crisp morning air had brought me back to normal—if anyone *could* be normal in this strange place.

I went back inside and stared at *the door.* It was wide open. I was sure that whatever was opening—and closing—the door wasn't human. *It* was much more powerful.

Wishbone stood in the darkened kitchen. He had stared at the cabinet for so long, he was beginning to see spots in front of his eyes. "Okay, let me run through this. . . . A dog alone in the kitchen on Halloween night . . . A cabinet door that slowly creaks open . . . Nope! Still can't explain it. Maybe I'll just go to bed."

228

Wishbone stood up, but he didn't walk away.

"What am I—a man or a mouse? I'm neither! *I* am a dog—my nickname is 'Courage'! I boldly go where no dog has gone before!" He stepped toward the cabinet, then pushed the door with his nose.

Something pushed from the other side of the door.

Clink-clink-clank!

"Hey!" Wishbone jumped back, the fur on his neck bristling. Whatever was inside the cabinet was moving!

You know, I can really relate to Phil, all alone in a great big house, not knowing what's going to happen next. Wishbone's nose twitched. *Hmm . . . I smell . . . something—it's gotta be a clue! I hope it's as good as the clue Phil is about to get at Ladlow Hall.*

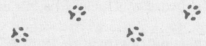

I went to my room and sat down. With pen in paw, I wrote a letter to Mr. Carrison, the man who had rented Ladlow Hall. I told him all about the broken spike. Then I wrote a letter to Patty and told her how much I missed her.

Taking both pieces of mail in my mouth, I trotted into the village to see the postmistress. I dropped the letters in her hand. "Good day." With a quick nod, I hurried right back to Ladlow Hall.

A basket had been left on the porch. In it was a card with my name on it! I lowered my nose to the basket and sniffed. Pumpkin cookies—yum! I wagged my tail, then took a bite of one of the cookies.

Suddenly, Lord Ladlow's warning about some-one wanting to poison my food stopped me in mid-bite. Why had I been so foolish to take even one bite? I didn't have a clue about who had brought the cookies!

My stomach began to roll. Right away I knew something was wrong. I started to see double. As quickly as I could, I ran to the lawn to get some grass to chew. Hot, cold. Hot, cold. I shivered. My head ached. I felt dog-tired. I trotted dizzily into the house and went down the hall to my room. I was sure I had been poisoned.

I dreamed about monsters . . . and Patty . . . and about Patty becoming a monster. She wanted to kill me! The dream was horrible. I cried out in my sleep and woke myself up. I was still alive! I thumped my tail weakly on the bed. I was lucky I hadn't eaten more of the cookies.

Slowly putting one paw in front of the other, I walked down the hall. My head still ached. Looking out one of the windows, I realized the sun was in the west. I'd been asleep for hours!

My strength was slowly returning. I went to fetch the basket from the porch, hoping to find a clue. But it was gone! *I'd better check the pantry to make sure my food is still safely locked up,* I thought.

As I passed through the kitchen, a beam of sun-light streamed in a window. Dust floated in the light like miniature snowflakes. All of a sudden my eyes were drawn to the floor, where the beam of light ended. A layer of dust had settled over the floor. Look-ing carefully around, I saw my own paw prints. But I saw other prints in the dust, too. And ghosts don't leave shoe prints.

I decided that when night came I would hide in the mysterious room where the open door was. *Why hadn't I thought to do that before now?* I wondered. *Deep in the bottom of my heart, had I been afraid all along—a scaredy-cat?*

I spent what was left of the day shutting *the door* each time I passed it, as I had done before. But I also treated myself to some digging exercise in the huge gardens.

After dinner, as bedtime neared and creepy night shadows swallowed Ladlow Hall, I got nervous. The moon hadn't risen yet. For some reason, the house seemed more quiet and deserted than ever before.

Taking a lighted candle from the hallway, I went to my room, as usual. I moved around, pretending to get ready for bed. Then I blew out the candle. But I didn't jump up on the bed to sleep. Instead, I crept down the hallway and through the open door. A chill of terror raced down my spine as I stepped into the room. *So I had been afraid all along!*

I stopped and listened. The air was still and silent. Then, making my way across the room, I nosed my way behind the velvet drapes, and sat down to wait.

I waited for what seemed like forever. Then I waited even longer! All four of my legs wanted to twitch, move, stretch. My side itched. *Have I picked up some fleas here? Don't move. Don't move. Don't move,* I told myself. *Oh, this is torture!*

Finally, a bird started to sing—it was almost morning! *Horray! This awful waiting is nearly over.*

My tail started to wag, but I forced it to be still. *Too bad I'm no closer now to solving the mystery than I was last night.*

Hey! Muffled footsteps alerted my senses. But they weren't coming from the direction of the open door. *Helllooo! What's going on?* My heartbeat quickened. I listened. The locked door that I could never open—the one I had thought was a closet—opened. Someone walked into the room.

I heard rustling. *A lady's skirts?* I wondered. I edged my muzzle from behind the drapes and peeked out. A shadowy figure—a woman—hurried across the room. Quietly, she shut the open door, then pulled a key from the folds of her skirts and locked the door. Glancing over her shoulder, she walked toward the cabinet. She pulled out another key, much smaller than the first. Then, with a quick glance around, she unlocked the cabinet.

I barely had time to pull my head back behind the drapes before she looked in my direction. My heartbeat thudded in my ears. Still, I could hear the doors of the cabinet open and close, the drawers slide in and out. And I heard papers rustle.

She must be looking for something—but what? I wondered. I heard a sound I didn't recognize. Slowly, I peeked out again from behind the drapes. There was more light now. The woman, dressed in black, carried the nearby chair over to the cabinet. She climbed onto the chair and dug deep into the highest shelves of the cabinet.

"Where *is* it?" she hissed, as she shuffled through the last of the papers.

Helllooo! It finally hit me. *She's searching for the will of Lord Ladlow's uncle, and the letter explaining why he took his wife* out *of the will. This woman must be the uncle's widow!*

I ran out from behind the drapes. The woman saw me and she jumped off the chair. I went for her high-buttoned shoe and held it in my teeth. I was *not* going to let her get away.

She pulled my fur and scratched my face. This woman was no lady—she was a wildcat! I growled and continued to hold my grip. Then she gave my ear a good, hard yank.

"Watch it!" I snapped at her hand. In that split-second, she was freed.

She headed for the door where she'd entered the room. I knew if she reached it, she would escape to wherever the secret passage led.

I ran in front of her and grabbed the bottom of her skirts in my teeth. She pulled at my collar. Somehow, she saw my revolver, pulled it out of my pocket, then fired wildly.

She missed! My heart pounded loudly.

Then she aimed the gun in my direction. Suddenly, her mouth opened and her face whitened.

I smelled her fear. I saw the look of terror in her eyes.

"See!" she cried, then threw the revolver at me and raced out.

I spun around as a bullet hit my shoulder. I saw that the door the woman had bolted and locked with a key now stood open wide. An awful figure—its hand held high—stood nearby. Then I saw no more.

I fell to the floor with a thump. The widow must have pulled the trigger as she threw the gun.

The next day the mail carrier looked into the house through the foyer windows and saw me lying helpless and bleeding. Somehow I'd crawled out of the room and collapsed on the cold marble floor of the hallway. The village physician came to the mansion immediately to patch up my shoulder.

The next day, when Lord Ladlow returned, I explained. "Break the cabinet to pieces. I'm sure your letter and the will are in there somewhere."

Ladlow sent for his lawyers, and the cabinet was smashed to bits. Between two thin boards were the letter and the will. As expected, Lord Ladlow had received everything his uncle had owned. His uncle's widow, I found out, was nothing more than a gold digger—someone after his money. She left the village the very day I was shot and never returned.

Lord Ladlow gave me a handsome reward. I bought a nice-sized farm far, far away from Ladlow Hollow. That's where my dear, sweet Patty and I now live. We have a very comfortable life, and there are never any bill collectors nipping at our heels. But sometimes, in the dark of night, when I think about Ladlow Hall, I don't want to be in a room alone.

Wishbone's nose twitched again. "Hey, I know that smell—ginger snaps!" He stepped right up to the cabinet. "Okay, who's trying to steal my treats?" Wishbone waited. "Not talking, huh?"

Wishbone nosed the cabinet door open.

He looked inside. "Whew!" On a shelf above him, an open box of ginger snaps had fallen over. "So that's what pushed the door open. And look at this. . . ." Two ginger snaps had fallen from the box and landed on the floor on end, between the door and the cabinet.

Wishbone wagged his tail as he picked up one of the ginger snaps in his teeth.

"So that's why the door wouldn't shut—ye olde ginger snaps!"

As he glanced around the dark kitchen, Wishbone heard another *creak*.

He grabbed the other cookie, then backed away. "You know, Halloween's been fun. But I think I've had enough tricks for one day." At the kitchen doorway, Wishbone turned, went down the hallway, and ran up the stairs. "I'll just eat my treats in bed, next to Joe—so he won't be scared!"

Tails of Terror

About the Authors

Including information about the classic authors and stories

About Brad Strickland

*B*rad Strickland is a well-known writer of young people's books, including many WISHBONE titles. He wrote the first two books in The Adventures of Wishbone series, *Salty Dog* and *Be a Wolf!* With Thomas E. Fuller, he co-wrote many WISHBONE Mysteries: *The Treasure of Skeleton Reef, Riddle of the Wayward Books, Drive-in of Doom, The Disappearing Dinosaurs,* and *Disoriented Express.* With his wife, Barbara, Brad co-wrote another book in The Adventures of Wishbone series: *Gullifur's Travels.* Brad also wrote *Jack and the Beanstalk,* the first title in the Wishbone: the Early Years series.

Brad has also penned a number of other mysteries for young readers, including *The Specter from the Magician's Museum* and *The Bell, The Book, and The Spellbinder.* He likes to read mysteries, fantasies, and science fiction.

Brad teaches English at Gainesville College, in Gainesville, Georgia. He and Barbara live near the college in a house crowded with pets, including ferrets, cats, and dogs. Recently, Brad's son, Jonathan, acquired a Jack Russell terrier named Falstaff, who is almost as much fun as his TV hero, Wishbone.

About Joseph Sheridan Le Fanu and "Green Tea"

Joseph Sheridan Le Fanu was born in Dublin, Ireland, in 1814. His family traced its background to the group of French Protestants called the Huguenots. He was also related to the famous playwright Richard Brinsley Sheridan.

Le Fanu trained to be a lawyer. However, he found his true calling in writing fiction. When he was very young, he began to write short stories. Many were mysterious and even a little spooky. After 1840, Le Fanu became a journalist and author. By the 1860s, he was well known as Ireland's major writer of fantastic fiction.

Among the many stories Le Fanu wrote is *Carmilla.* It was probably the world's most famous vampire novel before Bram Stoker's *Dracula* came along. He also wrote *Uncle Silas,* a story in which the ghoulies and ghosties may or may not be real. "Green Tea" is one of Le Fanu's many short tales of terror and the supernatural.

Le Fanu died in 1873, but he's still remembered as one of the few authors who, like America's Edgar Allan Poe or Germany's E. T. A. Hoffmann, loved to write of the strange, the weird, and the fantastic.

About Michael Anthony Steele

Michael Anthony Steele—or Ant, as he is known to his friends—loves spooky stories. In fact, when Ant was just a kid, he spent many a stormy night staying up late and reading scary stories and books. Then, of course, he had to stay up even a little longer after he had finished the stories since they were so frightening. Ant had a vivid imagination even when he was a boy. And sometimes a vivid imagination can keep you awake after you read a scary story.

During the second season of the WISHBONE television show, Ant worked as a staff writer and co-wrote the Halloween special, *Halloween Hound: The Legend of Creepy Collars;* the TV episode *War of the Noses;* and Wishbone's first movie, *Wishbone's Dog Days of the West.*

His other credits include the WISHBONE Mysteries titles *Forgotten Heroes* and *Case of the Impounded Hounds;* The Adventures of Wishbone title *Digging to the Center of the Earth;* the WISHBONE SUPER Mysteries title *The Ghost of Camp Ka Nowato;* and the script for the CD-ROM, *Wishbone Activity Zone.*

Ant lives with his wife, Becky, in Texas. The couple has a house full of animals. They have two Chihuahuas, Juno and Echo; a Staffordshire terrier, Odessa; and an English bulldog, Rufus. Ant and Becky also have two Siamese cats, Pluto and Bromius; a snake, Bishop; and an aviary full of finches and canaries.

Now on dark, stormy nights, Ant and Becky don't have to be frightened. They have plenty of dogs in the house to protect them—that is, except for Rufus, the bulldog. He's really scared of storms.

About Margaret Oliphant and "The Open Door"

Margaret Oliphant was born in Scotland in 1828. She moved to London, England, in 1850 and married Francis Oliphant in 1852. Her husband died in 1859 and left Margaret with three young children to support. She became a writer so that she could support her own family and the family of her widower brother.

Margaret wrote several novels and biographies. She also wrote several short stories for *Blackwood's Magazine.* Among those stories was a spooky tale called "The

Open Door." Oliphant wrote several books and stories that took readers into the realm of the supernatural. Many believe that those stories and books were some of Oliphant's best work. Of all of her spooky stories, some people believe that "The Open Door" is one of the finest ghost stories ever written.

Margaret wrote more than one hundred books and many stories. Some of her most well known books are *Caleb Field, Merkland, Passages in the Life of Mrs. Margaret Maitland,* and *The Athelings.* Her supernatural writings included a group of books called *Stories of the Seen and Unseen.* Two of the titles in this series are *A Beleaguered City* and *A Little Pilgrim in the Unseen.*

About Mary Ryan

*M*ary Ryan and her identical twin, Margaret, were born in Manchester, New Hampshire. They later moved to Tempe, Arizona. The sisters used to write poems, stories, and plays, which they would perform at school. (One production, *Dolty and the Dragon*, made the rounds of the entire fourth grade.)

Growing up, Mary had many cats, but only one dog—a plucky black-and-tan dachsund named Hercules (because he was the runt of the litter). Every summer the Ryan family would drive to New England and take all their pets with them. One year, Mary's cat got lost in Michigan. Found a week later, the feline spent the summer in Sheboygan, until the family picked him up on the way home. (The cat's name was Adventure!)

As the daughter of an art teacher and an English

professor, Mary always knew she wanted to write books (her first, created at the age of four, was an adaptation of *Winnie the Pooh*). After studying for several years in Europe, Mary graduated from New York University with a degree in filmmaking.

In New York City, she acted off-Broadway and even danced in a musical. However, she eventually decided it was more fun to write about those experiences. Her first book for children, *Dance a Step Closer*, was followed by five more, including *My Sister Is Driving Me Crazy* and *Alias*, which has been nominated for young readers' awards in California, Texas, Nevada, and South Carolina.

Mary attended Stanford University. Then she went to Seattle, Washington, where she earned a master's degree in English at the University of Washington. She still lives near the university, and now she runs her own word-processing business. Like Wishbone, Mary has been on TV—she was recently a contestant on the popular game show *Jeopardy!*. She played well and became a champion, winning prizes including a week in Hawaii. Mary is owned by a small black cat named Mickey, who supervises her every waking hour (and supplies a few of them himself!).

About Edward Bulwer-Lytton and "The Haunters and the Haunted"

Edward George Earle Bulwer-Lytton (1803-1873) was born in London, England. The son of wealthy parents, young Edward went to Trinity College, Cambridge. He began to write in order to support his expensive lifestyle. He wrote poetry, plays, and novels on many different subjects—ancient history, English royalty, the French Revolution, and even ghost stories and science fiction (H. G. Wells was influenced by his ideas). His best-known works are the historical novels *The Last Days of Pompeii* and *Rienzi;* and the plays *The Lady of Lyons* and *Richelieu.* Also a politician and critic, Bulwer-Lytton was a very popular writer, and in 1866 he was given the honorary title of Lord Lytton.

His ancestral home, Knebworth, is now a popular tourist attraction. Whenever he wrote, Bulwer-Lytton liked to dress up in elaborate robes and smoke one of his many pipes. He and his close friend Charles Dickens collaborated on several plays; in fact, Dickens's *A Tale of Two Cities* was modeled after his friend's novel *Zanoni.* Bulwer-Lytton waged a lifelong feud with the poet Tennyson, who accused him of being a fop and a dandy (an overdressed snob, which he was).

Bulwer-Lytton is also famous for writing such memorable lines as "It was a dark and stormy night . . ." (the opening of his 1830 novel, *Paul Clifford*) and "The pen is mightier than the sword," from the 1839 play *Richelieu.*

"The Haunters and the Haunted" (subtitled "The House and the Brain") has been described as the best ghost story ever written. Even in Bulwer-Lytton's time it was hailed as his masterpiece. Published in *Blackwell's Magazine* in 1857, it was expanded by the author into a novel, *A Strange Story,* in 1862.

About Nancy Holder

*N*ancy Holder is the author of thirty-eight novels for children, young adults, and adults; and more than two hundred short stories. By herself, and with her frequent writing partner, Christopher Golden, she has written a dozen books about Buffy the Vampire Slayer. She also writes books and short stories about Sabrina the Teenage Witch.

Many of Nancy's novels are about the supernatural, and she loves a good ghost story. While she read "The Portrait-Painter's Story," she felt chills running up and down her spine—on a bright, sunny day in San Diego, California! The mystery surrounding the origin of the two versions of the story made it even spookier for her.

Nancy is writing *Ivanhound*, for The Adventures of Wishbone series. It is based on *Ivanhoe*, a classic adventure story about chivalry and knighthood.

Nancy lives in San Diego with her husband, Wayne, and their daughter, Belle. They have two dogs, Mr. Ron and Dot. For many years, the family provided a "retirement home" for dogs that had once acted in movies and performed in theme parks. They would love to have Wishbone come live with them—if he ever gets tired of being famous!

About Charles Dickens and "The Portrait-Painter's Story"

Charles Dickens was born in southern England in 1812. When he was twelve, his family moved to London. His childhood was very unhappy and his family was poor. His father was thrown into prison because he

244

couldn't pay his debts. Charles had to leave school to work in a blacking warehouse (blacking was a kind of polish used to dye leather and other things).

Dickens learned important lessons from these early experiences. He worked very hard his entire life, even after he became rich and famous. Not only did he write, but he gave lectures and public readings, and he edited magazines. He felt great concern for poor people and wrote dozens of short stories and novels about them. His skill at making his readers care about his characters made him the most popular writer of his time.

Dickens also wrote many ghost stories, including *A Christmas Carol* and "The Portrait-Painter's Story." A shorter version of "The Portrait-Painter's Story" appeared in *All Year Round*, a magazine Dickens owned and edited. It was part of a collection of spooky tales called *Four Ghost Stories*. The four stories were published on September 14, 1861. A few days later, a man told Dickens that he was a portrait painter, and that the story had really happened—to him!

Dickens was amazed, because he had invented the story. He printed the portrait painter's more detailed version on October 5, 1861. In his magazine, Dickens told about the circumstances surrounding the story. Some people think Dickens actually wrote both versions.

Charles Dickens died in 1870. Some say his death was a result of working too hard. He had ten children with his wife, Mary, but their marriage was not a happy one. Yet by the time he passed away, he was beloved by readers all over the world.

About B. B. Calhoun

B. B. Calhoun wrote her first children's book, a collection of stories, when she was six. That special edition was just for her little sister. Since that time, she has written forty books for young readers, including the *Dinosaur Detective* series.

Before she became a writer, B. B. Calhoun was a teacher. She misses her students, but she loves writing books because it allows her to do something for kids and to make her own schedule. That means she and her daughter, Katie, have time to sit down and watch Wishbone every afternoon with their little white dog, Buya. B. B. thinks that Buya and Wishbone have a lot in common. Buya enjoys curling up to listen to a good book, as well as chewing, digging, and napping on her big *purple* chair. But Buya has yet to utter a single word to the family. She seems to have a lot to say to Wishbone, though, and often barks at the television when he is on the screen.

B. B. has always loved a good spine-tingling story. To write the Scottish story "Wandering Willie's Tale," she spread a tartan plaid blanket on her lap in front of the computer. Then she opened a tin of Scottish shortbread cookies. New York City, where B. B. lives with her husband and daughter, is a far cry from the Scottish Highlands, where Sir Walter Scott's tale takes place. But she does get to hear bagpipes every autumn. At a firefighters' monument just down the block from where the family lives, a special bagpipe band of firefighters, called the Emerald Society, marches in kilts and plays its music every year.

About Sir Walter Scott and "Wandering Willie's Tale"

Sir Walter Scott may have been Scotland's best-loved storyteller. Trained as a lawyer, Scott wrote poems, novels, history books, biographies, and even travel memoirs. He also invented a whole new kind of writing—historical fiction, which combined ordinary characters with important historical events.

Born in 1771, Scott became very sick as a young child, and he went to live on his grandparents' farm in the part of the countryside known as the Scottish Highlands. He spent the next several years there, recuperating and listening to the stories of the old Highlanders. During these years, he developed a love of Scottish folktales, legends, history, and songs. Scott continued to visit the area often. He finally settled there with his wife and four children. He wrote many stories and poems about the people of the Highlands. A lot of them were based on the history and legends he had learned as a child, including the historical adventure *Ivanhoe* and the poem-story *The Lady of the Lake*.

A generous host, Scott loved to entertain people. It was said that he never told the same story twice. He loved animals, and he had a special fondness for dogs!

"Wandering Willie's Tale" is one of the historical stories Scott wrote about the Highlands. Originally, it was part of a longer novel called *Redgauntlet*. *Redgauntlet* tells the stories of the generations of inhabitants of Redgauntlet Castle, including Sir Robert and Sir John. The tale of Steenie Steenson is supposed to have been told to a passing traveler by Steenie's descendant, Willie Steenson, a blind fiddler.

Scott felt his stories made Scots people feel proud of their language, their country, and themselves. As Scott's books became more popular, so did tartans (the traditional Scottish plaids), kilts, and bagpipes!

Sir Walter Scott kept writing stories until he died, in 1824. His great-great-great granddaughters still live in Abbotsford, his home in the Highlands.

About Joanne Barkan

Joanne Barkan was born in Chicago, Illinois. She first moved to the East Coast to go to college. Then she settled in New York City to work as a writer and editor. She and her husband live near Riverside Park, which runs along the Hudson River. Her husband works as a painter and sculptor.

Joanne is the author of more than one hundred books for children. These include two titles in The Adventures of Wishbone series, *A Tail of Two Sitters* and *A Pup in King Arthur's Court*. She's working on her first book in the WISHBONE SUPER Mysteries series, *The Riddle of Lost Lake*. She also writes about politics and economics for adults.

Joanne chose "The Phantom Coach" for *Tails of Terror* because she thought it was unusual, well written, and *really scary!* Then she discovered she had a mystery on her hands. Who was Amelia B. Edwards, the author of the story? It took several hours to track down the information on the Internet. The final discovery, however, made this Wishbone project particularly exciting and fun.

Joanne was delighted to find out about such a multitalented writer and daring nineteenth-century woman. Joanne also discovered that she and Amelia B. Edwards have something in common: the habit of working late at night, and often all night. Here's what Edwards wrote about it: "In summer-time, it is certainly delightful to draw up the blinds and complete in sunlight a task begun when the lamps were lighted in the evening." Joanne couldn't agree more!

About Amelia B. Edwards and "The Phantom Coach"

Amelia Ann Blanford Edwards was born in London, England, in 1831. Her father served as an army officer and then went into the banking business. Her mother was Irish. Amelia showed great talents when she was still very young. She was writing and illustrating her own stories by age four. One of her poems was published when she was seven. She had a story published when she was twelve.

Amelia B. Edwards went on to write poems, stories, and articles for many magazines and newspapers. She also wrote eight novels. One, called *Lord Brackenbury*, was so popular that the publisher reprinted it more than a dozen times!

The famous writer Charles Dickens first published Edwards's story "The Phantom Coach." It appeared in his magazine *All Year Round* in 1864. This story is sometimes called "The North Mail." The word *mail* in the title means a mail coach—a horse-drawn carriage used to carry mail from one town to another.

At the age of thirty, Edwards began taking trips and

writing about them. For example, she explored isolated regions of the Dolomite Mountains (which are part of the Alps) on mule. She wrote of her experiences in a book called *Untrodden Peaks and Unfrequented Valleys*. She illustrated the book with her own landscape paintings.

In the 1870s, Edwards took a trip that changed her life. She sailed far up the Nile River in Egypt. She spent six weeks at the Temple of Rameses II doing archeological work. She wrote about this adventure in *A Thousand Miles Up the Nile*. From then on, she devoted herself to preserving the great monuments of Egypt. She learned to read hieroglyphs and became an expert on ancient Egypt. She founded the Egypt Exploration Fund in 1883 which published the writings of explorers.

Edwards loved her work and put in long hours every day. She was also active in the campaign to win the right to vote for women. In 1889–1890, she went on a lecture tour in the United States. There she received honorary degrees from several universities. She died in 1892 in her country home in Somerset, England.

In 1968, an expert on ancient Egypt began writing a series of mystery novels under the name Elizabeth Peters. The detective in these popular novels is an Englishwoman who lived at the same time as Amelia B. Edwards. The novels take place in Egypt, and the detective is an expert on that country. Her name is Amelia Peabody. The influence of Amelia B. Edwards lives on!

About Carla Jablonski

*L*ike Bram Stoker, Carla Jablonski is much more than a writer. She also works in the theater as an actress and director. Appearing in plays has taken her to Edinburgh, Scotland, where she enjoyed reading the ghostly folklore of Great Britain, and seeing some of the (possibly) haunted ruins firsthand.

In The Adventures of Wishbone series she has written: *Homer Sweet Homer* and *The Legend of Sleepy Hollow*. She's also written one book for the Wishbone: The Early Years series, based on the fairy tale "The Sorcerer's Apprentice." Carla has also penned a Clueless book, *Southern Fried Makeover*. She has edited books for kids, and knows all about scary stories after working on several of R. L. Stine's *Give Yourself Goosebumps* books.

About Bram Stoker and
"The Judge's House"

Bram Stoker is most famous for having written *Dracula*. Ever since this classic book was published in 1897, its main character, Count Dracula, has been one of the world's favorite characters. There have been countless films, plays, and stories about Dracula, or works that have been influenced by him and Bram Stoker's imagination.

Bram Stoker was born in Dublin, Ireland. He was a sickly child and wasn't expected to live. He spent most of his childhood in bed reading books. He was fascinated by the Irish folklore his mother told him. This interest in folklore eventually led him to explore the superstitions about vampires and other supernatural creatures he used in his writing. He knew from an early age that he wanted to be a writer. He enjoyed doing research, and while he was working on *Dracula* he visited many of the locations he describes in the book. But he wasn't only a writer. Stoker worked as a drama critic and then as the manager of the Lyceum Theatre in London.

Although *Dracula* was the most famous of Bram Stoker's works, he wrote several novels and short stories, usually on supernatural themes. "The Judge's House" first appeared in 1891 in "Holly Leaves," the Christmas issue of a magazine called *Illustrated Sporting and Dramatic Life*. In the nineteenth century, many magazines published short stories, and ghost stories were very popular in England, particularly at Christmastime. Since then, "The Judge's House" has been reprinted in many anthologies of ghost stories. It still has the power to scare us today!

About Vivian Sathre

*V*ivian Sathre has written a dozen books for children. Five of them are WISHBONE books. For The Adventures of Wishbone series, she has written *Digging Up the Past* and *Dog Overboard!*. For The SUPER Adventures of Wishbone series, she has written *Wishbone's Dog Days of the West*. For the WISHBONE Mysteries series, she has written *Stage Invader*. Vivian has also written one title in the Wishbone: The Early Years series, based on the fairy tale "Hansel and Gretel."

"The Open Door," which was originally written

by Charlotte Riddell, is Vivian's first short story for WISHBONE. She compares writing this short story to enjoying a small but tasty snack between two bigger, meatier meals.

Vivian has read many scary stories and has enjoyed every one. But she never reads ghost stories at home alone on a dark, windy night when the lights could go out at any second. She likes funny stories more then!

Vivian loves both dogs and writing, so she has a lot of fun writing for the WISHBONE series. In her spare time, when she isn't working on a book or visiting a school, Vivian enjoys going to baseball games, basketball games, and the theater. She lives in the Seattle area with her husband, Roger, and their two nearly adult sons, Mitchell and Karsten. The family has two cats that act very much like dogs. Vivian's glad her own house is not haunted!

About Charlotte Riddell and "The Open Door"

When England removed the newspaper tax in the 1850s, magazine publishing became popular. So did ghost stories. And Charlotte Riddell, author of "The Open Door," was one of the most well known female writers of ghost stories at that time.

Many women wrote ghost stories during this period to help make money when their husband's salary was not enough to support the family. Perhaps that is why Charlotte Riddell wrote, too. In 1861 she began editing—and co-owned—*The St. James Magazine*. During this period she wrote some excellent ghost stories. In 1882, these stories were published in a collection titled *Weird Stories.* "The Open Door" was one of the stories included.

Besides writing short stories and co-owning and editing a magazine, Charlotte Riddell, who also wrote under the names Mrs. J. H. Riddell and F. G. Trafford, found time to write thirty novels before she died, in 1906.

Read all the books in the
WISHBONE™ Mysteries series!